T2185p

PARADISE LANE

William
Taylor

**SCHOLASTIC
HARDCOVER**

Scholastic Inc.
New York

Library of Congress Cataloging-in-Publication Data

Taylor, William, 1940–
Paradise lane.

Summary: When fifteen-year-old Rosie Perkins, an outcast at school,
saves the life of a baby opossum, she finds an unlikely friend and ally in
Michael Geraghty, a classmate who is her complete opposite.
[1. Opossums — Fiction. 2. Friendship — Fiction] I. Title.
PZ7.T2188Par 1987   [Fic]   87-9434
ISBN 0-590-41013-X

12 11 10 9 8 7 6 5 4 3 2 1   7 8 9/8 0 1 2/9

Printed in the U.S.A.   12

First Scholastic printing, October 1987

In memory of
Rosa Dorothea Taylor

Note

The bushtailed possum, *Trichosurus vulpecula*, is native to Australia. It was first introduced to New Zealand in the mid-nineteenth century and has spread to almost all corners of the country. Nocturnal and herbivorous, the possum has become a considerable pest and is widely hunted for its fur. A marsupial mammal, it is a distant relative of the North American raccoon.

Chapter One

Had she been walking at her usual pace, the small movement at the side of the road would not have caught her eye. However, today she had time to spare and was making the most of it.

The road was roughly metaled. Coarse gravel was applied in the spring of every second year when the previous load had been so ground into the mud that weeds and grass sprouted almost at will along the center and grew thick on the shoulders. She stopped, curious. In the verge of dust, stones and heat a small creature squirmed. At first she thought it was a rat and a shiver of revulsion drew her hands together as she cautiously moved forward for a closer look. The animal moved again and now she could see it more clearly. Rat-sized, rat-tailed, but thinner in the body. Honey-colored. It was a baby possum, a joey.

The girl moved, uncertain. First a step toward the animal, then away. What to do? She looked around as if searching for some answer. Ahead on the road she spotted the reason for the baby possum being there. Flattened, killed by a passing vehicle, was an adult possum. The mother.

The sight was common enough along this lane and the girl showed no reaction. Her gaze rested once more on the scrap of life at the edge of the road. It continued to move in a painful, slow-motion struggle. Through the leaves of the tree overhead, a ray of sunlight fell across the tiny creature's head and she saw that it faced an agonizing death. Grit and dirt covered its eyeballs and was blinked into the mucous, which encrusted the surrounding fur. Its mouth lay slackly open.

Undecided as to what to do, her lips pursed slightly and she frowned. Again she tried to move away from it. She couldn't. Within her she knew she had a responsibility to do something. Within her, she knew she could not take the simplest course — that of just walking away.

She knelt and extended a finger. She touched the small creature and knew with this action a commitment on her part had been made. The fate of the animal, one way or another, rested with her. But what to do? The sight, the feel of the thing repelled her. She gently ran her finger down the ratlike body and in response it extended a foreleg and instinctively wrapped its tiny claw around her finger.

The girl sat back on her heels and considered

her options. She could kill it. Anyone who had lived along this leafy, near-deserted road as long as she had knew what pests these animals were as they ranged fields and bush and home gardens in their indiscriminate search for the most tender shoots. Two or three possums could wreck a garden in just one night. She should kill it. Pest it may well be but it did not deserve a slow, lingering death under the hot sun. She looked around for a stick or stone suited to the task.

"Gonna kill it then?" The voice came from above her and the shock was such that she fell back onto the stones. Using one hand to balance herself, she quickly used the other to tuck between her knees the skirt she had hoisted up as she squatted in the dust.

"You what . . . ?" It was a squawk more than anything.

The boy dropped from where he had been perched above her, hidden on a low bough of an old beech tree. "Can't do it, eh? Let me have it and I'll knock it on the head for you."

She gathered herself and stood, roughly brushing the dust off her clothes, and positioned herself between the boy and the possum. "You'll do nothing for me — and anyway, I wasn't going to kill it."

"Just gonna leave it then, eh?" He laughed. "That's real cruel, that is."

"I wasn't going to leave it," she said.

"What then?" He threw himself onto the grass, plucked a blade and started to chew on it, all the while smiling, staring at her.

She knew he was taunting her. She looked into his mocking eyes and hated him. She had always hated him. The loathing she felt changed her resolve. "I'm taking it home," she said.

"That's sure to kill it," he said. "Just take a bit longer, that's all. Be sort of like torture . . . but don't worry, *you* won't feel it."

She would not let him get to her. "I'm taking it home," she repeated.

"Never really thought you'd be the sort to torture little animals . . . still, you never can tell." He laughed again. "Shows just how wrong you can be."

"I'm taking it home," she said for the third time. "I'm going to clean it, feed it, look after it."

"Torture it — you gonna torture it."

"Look after it," she said firmly, knowing she sounded far more certain than she felt.

"Won't survive. Be dead by morning — you'll see. Never survive at that size." He spoke knowingly.

"Yes, it will. It'll be all right, I know it will." She wanted to stop talking. She wanted him to go.

"It's not even half grown, nowhere near it," he said. Again he laughed. "Aw, go on, let me kill it for you."

"I'll let you do nothing for me. And you'll not touch the possum." She bent down, swallowing her revulsion at handling the tiny creature, and picked the possum up. She breathed deeply. The baby possum resisted her hold. Fitfully, weakly, it tried to escape. She cradled it close to her and with this action it ceased its struggle and clung in the folds of her clothing.

"It'd be better off dead," said the boy. "Most things'd be better off dead than with you." He gave a short laugh and jumped up. "Don't say I didn't warn you — it'll be dead by morning, mark my words. And what's your old lady going to say? Can't see her wanting a possum!" He looked at her hopefully, waiting for a reaction. Getting none, he shrugged, and with a couple of steps and a jump he cleared a fence covered in blackberry bushes and was off into the trees on the hill.

Alone now, she felt less sure than ever. Had he not been there the possum would have been dead by now. A short, sharp blow of grace. The baby animal stirred within her hold. Its stirring, its delicate but determined cling to life reassured her.

A commitment had been made.

Rosa Dorothy Perkins, called Rosie, walked on home, wondering along the way how she could help the survival of the scrawny, dirty little creature. Maybe he had been right and it would die in the night. Not if she could help it.

Being a country girl, Rosie realized from the size of the baby possum that it still would have been dependent on its mother. Probably, she thought, it still suckled. Nothing she could do about that! She smiled to herself.

Old Dump Road was a rough, gravel road, little more than a track really, that snaked around a series of small hills, at times almost looping back on itself. Once, the road had led to the town dump but that was long ago. The gully that had received the garbage of the town for twenty or more years had long been filled in and deserted for another site. But the name stuck. Dump Road it had been; Old Dump Road it now was. Maps of the town actually showed its proper name as Paradise Lane. Leafy, cool and shady in summer, freezing cold in winter — it didn't quite live up to its name. Rubbish dump or paradise, it had not proved popular for settlement. There were only two houses along its entire winding length.

A short, cross-country distance separated Rosie's place from the town and occasionally she would cut through this shorter route. Not today, though. She needed the twenty minutes' worth of road. She needed the time to think what on earth to do with the baby possum.

The young of anything requires warmth, she knew that. But she could hardly put it in the oven and turn the switch to "low"! She thought she would try the hot-water cupboard.

Food? No option but to warm some milk for it. Or water? Maybe water would be better. Her hand registered the smallness of the animal. It was very likely dehydrated. He was right, damn him. He was right — it would die. Cow's milk and a box in a warm place were no substitute for a proper possum mother.

It was after five when Rosie turned in at her gate. She sighed. What on earth had she done? The last, the very last thing she needed was an almost dead possum to deal with.

The kitchen was empty. She found an old shoe-box, a towel, and with little ceremony and none too gently she shoved the possum into the box and deposited the lot in the hot-water cupboard.

Thinking of what attention she would need to give the possum later, she turned her hands to the job of preparing dinner for her father and herself. He would be home at six-thirty and dinner would be ready. It was Thursday. On Thursdays it was sausages. Sausages with potatoes, cabbage or carrots and frozen peas. Seldom any change from the pattern.

At six o'clock she checked on her mother. The curtains were drawn in her mother's room and she called softly, "Are you awake?" There was no response. "Do you want me to get you some dinner?" A slight stirring on the bed, nothing more. Again Rosie called, "Do you feel like any dinner?" Her eyes grew accustomed to the dim light. On the cabinet beside the bed the bottle of sherry was less than half full.

Michael Joseph Geraghty ran all the way home. He seldom used the road and the tracks of the hills were so familiar to him that he thought nothing of his path as he sprinted. He thought instead of Perkins and her possum. He hoped it died. He hoped its dying would well and truly upset Perkins.

He should have killed it. He had spotted it, too, almost at the same time she had. Her arriving, there and then, had saved it. Saved it for what? Dead by morning and serve her right. Sure would be happier dead. Could anything be happier dead? He thought that one over as he ran. Might sound funny, but he knew what he meant.

To Michael Geraghty, possums meant money. Possums meant income and livelihood. Time wasted on Perkins had kept him from skinning the fine, big buck and the smaller one that had been hanging in his possum shed since he had cleared his trapline that morning.

He hurried on through the shelter belt of tall macrocarpa trees that criss-crossed the wasteland. All this was his country, not hers. The tracks, the trees and the wildlife were his, not hers. As far back as he could remember, Old Dump Road had been his. Once he had shared it with his brothers but that was when he had been little and had tagged along behind. Now, with them all grown and gone, it was his — all his. That the Perkins had lived on the road as long as the Geraghtys had didn't matter at all. It was his, not hers.

She couldn't stand the sight of him. So what? He felt the same way about her. Everyone did. No one, no one at all could stand the sight of Perkins. Never could and never would. None of his mates, that was for sure. Big, pale green eyes she had, and all that long, fair, stringy, straight hair. Always looking and sounding as if she thought she was something different, something better. Better? Ha! That's a laugh! She'd never, ever had a friend and not likely to get one either. Always trying to make it look as though she couldn't care less.

Better? Hardly. Might be a walking textbook

on just about everything but she only lived on Old Dump Road, same as he did. What about her mother, then? Biggest drunk in town! Everyone knew.

"I sent you for sugar," said his mother. "Where on earth is it? And where on earth have you been all this time? Been quicker to go myself. Really, Michael — you knew I wanted to get these peaches done before they go off."

And there went another half hour and all because of Perkins. Michael trekked back to the tree where he had rested halfway home. He picked up the sugar from where he had left it beneath his perch. It was all Perkins' fault. Perkins and her stupid possum. He cursed out loud at the thought of the girl and the creature.

Chapter Two

"How's my Princess, then?" This time she was not quick enough to avoid the bear hug that followed. She held herself still inside his prickly embrace. Well practiced, she escaped from her father's grasp as the hug altered to a fondling and stroking of her hair.

"All right," said Rosie. "I'm all right. Dinner's ready."

He came toward her a second time but she was too quick for him, escaping to the other side of the table in a hasty laying of places and setting out of cutlery. "Of course it's ready," he mumbled. "It always is. What would Daddy do without his little Princess?"

Rosie made no reply and busied herself with getting food from stove to table and serving it onto three plates. The third plate — that of her mother — was for little more than show. Taken to her in her room, the food would sit, uneaten and ignored, to be got rid of, cold and fatty, the next morning. For a long time it had been done this way. A part of the game and of the pretending.

"How was school?" her father asked as they ate. "What did you do today?"

"Same as usual on a Thursday," replied Rosie. She tried to think of enough to say to stop up the hole of silence in their eating. "We got back our last math test."

"And how did Princess do?"

"I got ninety-three."

"What out of?" he persisted.

"Percent."

"Good, good, good. Very good." He beamed at his daughter. Reg Perkins was a solid and thickset man. Grey eyes; a steel grey. Grey hair, and still a full head of it even now in his mid-fifties. Steel grey hair. Just like his eyes. The face of the man was not unpleasant but it had a grimness to it that was only ever lightened by the sight of his daughter. "Ninety-three, eh? If you ask me, that's pretty good."

She could think of no reply to that. She thought of telling him about the baby possum but decided against mentioning it just yet. She realized with a little pang of guilt that she had almost forgotten it was stored in the hot-water cupboard.

"I'll check on your mother," said her father,

"then I'll get off back down to the shop for a while — a spell of fine weather and every mower in town seems to break down."

Why was it always "your mother," wondered Rosie. Why could he never refer to her as his wife? It was as if no relationship existed in the house other than that between the woman and the girl or the man and the girl. But nothing that linked all three.

She set about the dishes and tidying away the odds and ends of dinner, thinking first of her mother and father and then drawing her thoughts back to the animal that awaited her attention.

Probably dead by now, she thought as she dragged the shoebox from the cupboard. Almost, it was. The possum had moved from the old towel and lay curled on the bare cardboard of the box. It had soiled itself and there was a faint, unpleasant smell to it. Almost a smell of decay — in the process of death but not quite giving up to it. Rosie held the box in the crook of her arm and prodded at the creature. Again it curled to her touch. She put the box on the kitchen table and sat down to think of what to do.

Should she kill it? A quick thought, and just as quickly she rid herself of the idea. She didn't think it was truly within her to perform the actual killing deed. That sort of thing could be left to the likes of Michael Geraghty who seemed to take great joy in dispatching the defenseless. Besides, it would also mean that her rescue efforts would have been for nothing. Already there existed a small pact on her part, to ensure the survival of the baby possum.

She sat and thought. She knew that the prime needs of any living creature were food and shelter. Clothing? Well, in this case there was another need before she even got around to the prime ones. It needed a bath. Would its mother have cleaned it? Licked it? Well, she thought, there was no way she was about to imitate that!

Rosie got a cloth and a bowl of warm water. From the bathroom a drop, no more, of her own shampoo which she added to the water. The possum made no protest as she carefully gave it a sponge bath. As gently as possible, she cleaned around its eyes, its mouth and around its hindquarters where its own dirt had become further encrusted with the dust and grit of the road. By the time she had finished, it looked more dead than ever. Slightly alive, very damp, scarcely moving.

Animal fur contains oils. Rosie took a small amount of olive oil from a bottle she ferreted from the back of a kitchen cupboard and smeared it over the possum. "Lick it off if you want," she said. "If you know how to lick, that is. Just could stop you from getting whatever kind of pneumonia possums get."

It looked more rat than possum. Skinnier than ever, but at least it was clean. The possum gurgled, gagged and rejected most of the milk she prepared for it. Watered down, warmed and with a few grains of sugar, Rosie knew it must be quite unlike that of its mother. However, it was the best substitute she could come up with. She hoped that a few drops of the formula made it from eye-dropper to stomach.

Cleaned and fed; still deader than dead.

Placing it back on a clean corner of the towel, she sat back and thought again of shelter and clothing. Clothing? Nature had provided part of the solution by giving it a fur coat. A marsupial, Rosie guessed it was still at the stage of living, part-time at least, in its mother's pouch. Rosie had an inspiration.

An old coat of her mother's had hung for years at the back of the garage. Being of a furlike fabric, it just might provide an answer. She got the garment and, with scissors, hacked a panel from the back. From this she roughly fashioned and then stitched a pouch, fur side in. Did mother possums have fur-lined pouches? She didn't know. At any rate, they would be of the real thing and not artificial leopard skin! Still, it would have to do.

The possum was beyond protest when she picked it up and stuffed it feet first into the pouch. It rested there limply, damply, head poking out. Rosie lined a small apple box with some more of the fabric, placed the enveloped possum on this and bent a scrap of chicken wire across the top and down the sides. She did not bother securing it further. "I doubt if you're going to escape, little possum. I doubt you'll even survive . . . not even live through the night. Now, possum, I've done my best. The rest's up to you."

14

She cleared a high shelf in the hot-water cupboard. Warm air rises, she reasoned. Bending back the wire netting, Rosie made a further effort to force a few drops of eyedroppered liquid down the animal's throat, then deposited the box on its shelf and closed the cupboard door. Then she opened it again and looked in, as if to check that the contents of the box were still there.

"Possum," she said out loud, "it's all over to you now. Either you make it or you don't. Simple as that. No different, really, than it is for any other creature that lives and breathes." She peered into the box. "Seems to me, we all got to make it on our own. So what? You ended up without your mother. You've still got me and I've done my best to care for you. Might even work out better than a mother. Look at it this way — at least I'm less likely to get squashed on a road. Least I'm here and doing something for you. Squashed on a road? Huh! Sure not much different from always being zonked out in bed."

She slid the box back onto its shelf and closed the door again. "What about a father, then? Least you don't have that." Rosie laughed a dry little laugh. "Some old buck possum on some dark night. In, out and off — gone for good. God, possum, you don't know how lucky you are. You just thank your lucky stars."

Michael Geraghty worked on the large, brown-red buck he had caught that morning. His eight or nine traps usually yielded a harvest of one, sometimes two, and occasionally a bonus of three

15

or four beasts. In the mornings before school, before breakfast even, while the rest of the household slept, Michael was up, dressed against the weather and checking if the night had given him anything.

Old Dump Road marked the edge of a sizeable hinterland, a no-man's-land of waste ground on the outskirts of town. With its scrubby bush and inferior pine, seldom disturbed by more than a few trail-bike riders or rabbit shooters, it was common ground. Not overinfested with possums, there were nevertheless enough to warrant the activity of Michael and one or two others. The price for skins was good.

"Set traps if you want," his father had said, "but there are one or two rules if you're going into possums. You'll do it properly or not at all. You can use the old shed down the back." It was well away from the house. "You'll check your traps every morning, no matter what the weather's like. Catch the devils if you want, but I won't have a boy of mine leave any animal to suffer for too long. You can hang them for that day and no longer — and bury the remains. Understood?" Michael had understood. "Don't expect to make your fortune. Your brothers didn't and nor will you. You'd do better with a paper run. Still, I guess you're old enough to know your own mind."

"And if I catch one whiff of possum on you," his mother had added, "that'll be an end to it. Sort out your oldest clothes to wear, and make sure you shower afterwards."

There was little he hadn't known about the

business. Ever since he could remember he had followed after his older brothers and had looked, learned and often done the least pleasant of possuming jobs. He was determined to show his father that he could make more from his industry than if he had taken on a paper run. He'd show them all that he could make good money, and he wanted to save.

The morning catch had been satisfactory. The one good buck was a perfect deep and rusty red. It'd bring a good price. The smaller one was a young grey. Two possums. From start to finish it would take little more than half an hour. He could do it more quickly but it wasn't worth it. The effort taken now would make all the difference between a good price and next to nothing.

Michael sleeve-skinned the animals. He worked with a swiftness and economy of movement that came with experience.

After skinning both animals he disposed of the bodies before returning to his furs. Using an old spoon he scraped the insides clean of fat and finished the process by rubbing the skins down with a rough towel. From a collection of boards he selected those he estimated would fit the pelts and slipped each through the inside-out fur sleeves. Quickly and efficiently he secured the skins to the boards with spring pegs. Finally, the boards were hung along with a score of others similarly prepared and in various stages of drying.

Michael tidied what little mess remained and carefully bolted the door of the shed against the possibility of rats. One rat could ruin an entire collection of drying skins and lay waste a whole season of hard work. From time to time he laid poison or traps under the little building, or encouraged Hitler, his old black cat, to patrol the precincts. In his old age, Hitler was none too keen to be drafted to any duty.

Michael glanced at his watch. He was late and his mother's call to dinner confirmed this. Silently he cursed Perkins. Ugly Perkins. All her fault, most definitely. If it had not been for her and her possum he'd have been done an hour since. In no way could it be his fault for sitting and idling away the time in a summer-leafed tree.

Michael Geraghty was fooling with a group of his friends outside the science lab when he spotted Rosie Perkins walking toward them. He whispered quickly and quietly to the group then called, "How's your dead possum, Perkins?"

She was walking alone. She usually did. She did not respond to his call. Her quiet ignore stung the group.

"Got a dead possum, Perkins?" called one.

"Collects them," jeered Michael.

"Better keep an eye out, Mick — she'll be nicking your traps next. Or she'll want to go into partnership!" Loud laugh.

She was passing in front of them.

"Perkins got a possum," said one.

"Perkins got a *dead* possum," said Michael. "How's your dead possum, Perkins?"

"Possum Perkins," called another.

"Possum Perkins!" They started a chorus. "Possum Perkins! Possum Perkins!"

Rosie stopped. "Curiously enough . . ." she began.

"Curiously enough," Michael mimicked.

"Possum Perkins, Possum Perkins, Possum Perkins . . ." His friends accompanied him.

"Curiously enough," Rosie started again, "it's alive and quite well. It's coming on nicely." She finished uncertainly.

"Coming on nicely. Coming on nicely. God, listen to her," said one of Michael's friends. "Shoulda got it first, Mick. Stretched its neck. Better a stretched neck than living with Perkins."

"With any of the Perkins."

"Possum Perkins, Possum Perkins . . ." Their cries followed her down the corridor. As she walked away from them there was nothing about her that showed their taunts meant anything at all.

Chapter Three

Rosie Perkins' possum survived. Within a week it became clear to Rosie that she could no longer expect it to stay quiet and passive within its home-made pouch. Nor could it be hidden away for very much longer in the hot-water cupboard. She still had little idea of how to set about rearing it in the long term. A search of both town and school libraries had not proved to be of any help in the matter.

What little information she could find told her it was at about the halfway point between birth and full growth. This was not of much use, given that a marsupial is born while still an embryo and that this joey had been less than fingernail size at birth and had then made the perilous journey upwards through its mother's fur to eventually arrive in her pouch. Here it had found and attached itself to her teat.

Rosie could only guess that her possum had reached the stage of leaving its mother's pouch for at least part of the time, still returning regularly to suckle and sleep. She continued its milk diet and tried it on odds and ends of other foods. At this stage, however, it showed no interest in anything other than the milk she gave it. Gradually, too, it seemed to recognize in the girl if not a mother then at least some presence that was interested in caring for it. Equally gradually, the caring that Rosie gave became less a duty and more because the young animal responded to her. Rosie found that she cared.

On the third day she had named the possum. She called it Plum. In color it was identical with the fruit now ripe on the old tree at the back door. And when the possum rolled into a ball, well, with her eyes squinted, it even looked a bit like a plum. Anyway, it isn't all that easy to find a satisfactory name for a possum.

During Plum's second week in the cupboard it became clear to Rosie that the secret could no longer be kept. Arriving home one day she went immediately to feed and check on her pet. It had escaped from its box but was not difficult to find. A trail of droppings littered the shelf and dotted the oddments of stored linen. Plum came immediately to Rosie's outstretched hand and she spoke sternly to the animal. "You bad thing. You're a bad, bad thing. Stay in your box now and I'll get you some milk. It'd be the end of you if you

21

got out of here. You wouldn't last one night, you know that?" Pausing, she added, "And after all I've done for you!"

That evening at dinner with her father, in a quiet moment while he digested his carrot-speckled savory mince and her latest science score, she said, "I've got a possum."

"You what?" He sounded puzzled. "In science, was it?"

"No, no. Not in science," she said. "I've got a possum I found. It's just a baby." It came out in a rush.

"You can't have a possum. You can't keep a possum. They don't make pets, possums. Besides, your mother won't have pets. Allergic to them, she is."

"I found it on the road a week — no, two weeks ago. Nearly two weeks ago."

"You can't keep a possum," he repeated.

"But I have kept it," replied Rosie. "I've been keeping it up till now and it's survived."

"What does my Princess want with any silly old possum? It won't live. And what if it does?"

She smiled at him — appealed to him. "I think it would be a good idea to see if I could rear a possum. I've already started to write it up as an experiment," she lied. "I want to find out if it's possible to raise a possum, a baby one, away from its mother. I'd like to see if it keeps its possum characteristics." She lied again. "I've talked it over with our science teacher and he says it would be an interesting and worthwhile thing to do." How easy it was for one lie to lead to another.

22

Her father pursed his lips. "Don't want possums around here. Damn nuisance that they are. Still, seeing as how it's for school . . ." He paused. "Well then, just for a while, you can give it a go."

"Thank you, Daddy." She rewarded him with a small smile. "I knew you'd understand."

"Anything for my girl," he said. "Don't know for the life of me where you'll keep it. And your mother . . ."

"I've got it all worked out. Nothing for you or Mummy to worry about, I promise. I'm going to keep it in that little storeroom at the back of the garage. She never goes in there and neither do you. I'll clean it out and make a cage for it and look after it and everything. I will, I promise."

"What if he escapes?"

"It's a she. She won't," said Rosie.

"You seem very certain," he said. "Well, it'll be our little secret then, Princess. Come on now — give your old man a kiss and say thank you nicely. We won't bother telling your mother, now will we? Then I'll give you a hand to fix it all up."

"It's all right, Daddy, really it is. I should do it myself. As part of the experiment, sort of." She braced herself and gave her father as quick a kiss as she could get away with. She allowed herself to be held momentarily without trying to break away.

"There's my clever Princess, then," he said, stroking her hair before letting her go.

Plum adjusted to the new home and seemed to make full use of the habitat created for her by Rosie. The possum continued to use the false pouch, but more and more often ranged the extent of what was, in reality, just a much bigger chicken-wired box. Rosie fed her in the mornings and again in the afternoons and began leaving a saucer of water and vegetable scraps for the creature to eat during the day. However, for quite some time Plum continued to prefer a milk diet.

In the evenings Rosie would take Plum out and play with her. A relationship was growing between them. Her father made no further mention of the animal. He appeared to have forgotten about it.

Michael Geraghty and his two closest friends decided Rosie Perkins was well and truly ripe for further torment. They hit upon what they considered to be an excellent idea that would really fix her.

"She's got it coming to her. Weirdo," said Calvin.

"Always thinking she's better'n anyone else," said Fred.

"Need something that'll get up her nose real good. Stuck up cow," added Michael.

"She's your next-door neighbor," Cal reminded him.

"What's that got to do with it? S'pose you're blaming me for that!" said Michael.

They gave up on the idea of a dead possum in her desk. There would be little doubt about where the blame would fall.

They knew the joey had survived. Answering a question in class on how to care for the abandoned young of wild creatures, Rosie had briefly and clearly outlined what she was trying to do with Plum. Michael, Calvin and Fred considered the idea of a raid on the Perkins home.

"You oughta have a good idea where she'd keep it, Geraghty," said Fred. "We sneak in, possum-nap it, knock it on the head, then post it back to her in a parcel."

The thought of Mr. Perkins, large and bearlike, catching them in the process of their raid, much less Rosie or her loony mother, soon persuaded them that other methods, far less hazardous to themselves, could possibly be even more rewarding.

On Old Dump Road they set their trap. "She'll never want to see another possum after this," said Cal. Michael secretly thought to himself that after this he just might not want to either. The payoff had better compensate for the foulness of the job.

They had scouted and scoured the roads around the town, collecting the bodies and remains of four possums that had been run over, killed by traffic. Not all were fresh fatalities.

The tree beneath which Rosie had discovered Plum seemed the ideal setting. The branches of the old beech swept well across the road at a short distance above the height of pedestrian heads or passing vehicles. The leaves were summer thick and the branches wide enough to make a satisfactory platform. They strung up their trophies of the road, balancing them in such a way that a jerk on two cords from their hiding places in the recesses of the old tree would tumble the carcasses

onto the road beneath. It wasn't the road, however, that they intended showering. It was the
head of Possum Perkins.

They lay in wait, poised in their lair, anticipat-
ing the reaction of their victim. She didn't come.

"You reckon she always comes this way, Geraghty," moaned one.

"She does."

"Sure doesn't look like it. Less we're all blind."

"Be patient." Michael looked at his watch, puzzled. Regular as clockwork, she traveled this road.
He hadn't known her to go cross-country for
months. What could have gone wrong? She
couldn't have known what they were up to, what
was waiting for her . . . could she?

Ten minutes. Twenty minutes. Half an hour.

"She's not coming."

"You said . . ."

"Look. Ninety-nine times out of a hundred she
does. Okay? So, this time she hasn't. Doesn't matter. We'll leave it all set up for tomorrow. Possums'll stink that much better for another day.
Something's happened this time, that's all. We can
all come tomorrow. No sweat. Anyway," continued Michael, looking at his watch again, "I gotta
go now. I've got Bible Class tonight and me old
lady'll murder me if I'm late." They left their trap.

Some time later, fully unsuspecting of what
waited above her, Rosie drove beneath the tree
with her father. The one time out of a hundred
had been a visit to the dentist.

The next day was different. Hot, clear and very

fine and a less than delicate odor rising from their bait.

"If she don't come today, Geraghty," threatened Calvin, "you're gonna get this little lot smacked round your face."

"She'll come," said Michael curtly.

She did. At a good pace and swinging her school bag. The sun danced lights in her long, blonde hair.

"Jeez, she's strange. Did you see her in math today? Jeez . . ."

"Shut up," said Michael.

They sprung their trap and the plan worked with a perfect simplicity. Rosie was caught in midstride. Two of the carcasses fell, hitting her as they plummeted to the ground. The other two, on shorter rope, jerked and dangled, puppetlike, grotesque, in front of her. She screamed in fright and disgust and attempted to ward off the pendulum swing of the dangling bodies.

The three boys leapt from their perch shrieking with delight, as much at the success of their plan as at her obvious distress.

"Ha! Got you, Perkins!"

"Possum Perkins, Possum Perkins . . ."

"How about bringing these ones back to life, eh, Perkins?"

"Give 'em mouth-to-mouth, Perkins!"

"Possum Perkins, Possum Perkins. Have a possum, Possum Perkins."

Over and over and over again, it seemed to her. On and on. She backed off slightly and half turned to face her tormentors. "You bastards!" Her voice stilled them. "You revolting, despicable bastards!" She gulped harshly. "You horrible, horrible, cowardly swine. No, not swine. There's nothing wrong with swine. You're all sick. Sick! Sick! Sick!" She yelled at them, heedless of the danger of being one against three. She screamed her anger at them, her revulsion outweighing any other consideration. "You're not animals. You're not human. God! I don't know what you are. You, you . . . you're creeping, little evils . . . slimes. . . ." Her face twisted and flashed with a fire they had never seen. Then she was still. Suddenly still. Stone still and silent.

"Aw, shut up, Perkins."

"Teach you a good lesson . . ."

"Reckon you're so smart, eh?"

"Possum Perkins, Possum Perkins."

Jeering. More jeering. Then something burst their balloon of excitement. "Come on. Let's get outa here. . . ." Little more than a mumble.

"Leave the cow . . ."

"Gotta get home . . ."

"Me old lady . . ."

They edged away with an unease and disquiet caused in part by Rosie's sudden stillness. Rosie said nothing. She did not move.

The boys slunk off, up and down the road, taking separate paths into the greenery, leaving the girl with their grisly gift.

Michael, alone now, doubled back on his track, returning to the place on the road where they

28

had left Rosie. He did not know why he went back. Maybe it was no more than idle curiosity at seeing again the havoc their act had wrought. He came back down the slope of old trees and onto the road. He approached quietly and stood where he was able to see but remain unseen.

Of the possum bodies there was now no sign. The string still hung from the tree but there was nothing hanging from the cords. To one side, on the bank of the road, lay Rosie Perkins. She sobbed with a wild grief. Face down in the grass, her body was racked with fierce, jerking movements. She did not see him.

He stood, shocked at the sight. Her body rocked continuously. Clearly, she was not aware that anyone might be watching. She was heedless. Michael moved toward her without any clear idea of what he might do. She did not notice him as she rocked back and forth. Tentatively, unsure, he knelt down and touched her on the shoulder. She sprang up and away at his touch, her eyes scanning the area around and behind where he stood, searching for the others, as if expecting them to have come back for another round of fun.

"It's . . . it's only me," he stammered.

"Get out! Get away! Go on, get lost!" Her voice was low and she spat the hard sounds of the words right at him. "Leave me alone. Get out!"

"I'm sorry. I'm sorry, Rosie."

She recognized from the tone of his voice, his manner, that she was safe from further attack. She quieted, exhausted. "Get out. Go on. Get away from me," she muttered.

29

"I — I — we — I never thought . . ."

"Never thought?" she spat back at him. "I doubt if you and your friends ever think, ever. Not of anything at all. Now go! Go on, get away."

"What did you do with — er — you know . . ." he mumbled.

"With the possums? The dead possums? Want their skins, do you? Is that why you came back? Or was it that you thought I couldn't get rid of them. Couldn't touch them. Is that it?"

She seemed to have quieted, he thought. He risked himself again. "I am very sorry, Rosie. I — we shouldn't have done what we done. Just shouldn't have."

"You can sit there and grunt sorry for the rest of your life. I don't care what you do! I don't give a damn." She warmed slightly to what she was saying and again he caught a glint in her expression. "You just sit there, for all I care, sit there working out the next thing to kick me with. Maybe next time you and your pathetic boyfriends will have enough guts to do something to me yourselves and not leave it to four rotten-dead possums to do your dirty work. Guts! Huh! What a laugh! One dead possum's got more than the three of you put together. Now, get out!"

She left him. He watched as she moved away up the road. If he hadn't known otherwise, it was almost as if nothing had happened to her. The same sun lit sparks into the same blonde hair as when she had approached the tree an hour ago, before it all happened.

30

He stayed there, staring into the leaves for a long time. Finally, he climbed the tree and removed the dangling cords. A reminder he'd prefer not to see as he passed up and down the road. Then, Michael walked home.

Chapter Four

"Leave it!" said Michael abruptly the next day
when Cal and Fred gathered an audience to tell
of the success of their venture. "Just drop it, eh?
We shouldn't have done it."

"What's got into you? Deserved it, she did. Had
it coming in heaps."

"Shut up," said Michael.

"It was your idea in the first place, Geraghty,"
said Cal, reasonably. "Me? I couldn't care less what
happens to the cow."

"And stop calling her a cow," said Michael.

Something in his tone warned the other two.
Fred raised an eyebrow at Cal and shook his head.
"Bit late to be worrying about what we done, Mick,"
he said quietly.

"Shouldn't have done it. No way," repeated Mi-

32

chael. "Was a bloody awful thing to do to anyone." The tone of his voice told the others that was the end of the matter.

Michael did his best to avoid Rosie all day. At one stage he caught her eye but not by the flicker of a lash did she show that she saw him. No matter how hard he tried, it seemed to him that no matter where he went as they moved around the school that day, period by period, she was always there. Quiet as ever. And it was as if this ignore was all directed at him. It was stupid. After all, they had never spoken to each other, anyway.

Deliberately, that afternoon, he waited for her, sitting beside the road but further up from the place of the events of the day before. He had to talk to her. Didn't know why, but he had to talk to her. Nor did he know what on earth he would say. He positioned himself in the open so that she would see him quite clearly and know that he was alone.

Rosie approached. She saw him sitting there but did not break stride. She did not slow nor even indicate that she had noticed him. She moved straight on ahead. As she came abreast of him he stood and spoke to her. "I want to talk to you." She stopped, looked at him and said nothing. She began to move on again. "Please," he said, very quietly. "I'm all by myself."

"I can see that," she answered. "You mean you want to talk to me?"

"Yeah. That's what I said. I have to."

"Well, I don't have to talk to you. I don't want to talk to you. You've been following me round all day and I don't like it. Why have you been following me round all day?" She shrugged. "Not that I care. Besides, I have to get home."

"Just for two minutes, that's all," he pleaded.

She said neither yes nor no but put her bag down on the bank and sat down beside it. She looked at him.

"I've got to say that I'm very sorry — very, very sorry — for what happened yesterday. It's the worst thing I ever done. It was sick. Real sick. You can't blame the other two. It was all my idea — they just came along. My mother'd kill me if she ever found out. She'd be so ashamed," he mumbled. The words would not come out as he had practiced them.

"So you're sorry because of what your mother might think? Scared I'm gonna tell her?" Rosie asked. "Is that it? Is that what you're worried about?"

"Yes. I mean no. I don't know. I've just got to say sorry for me and what I done."

"Did," said Rosie.

He ignored her correction. "Look, I can promise you it won't ever happen again — it won't ever happen again."

"Well, I really didn't think it would," said Rosie. She continued slowly. "Even you'd get tired of collecting decaying possums and sticking them up a tree. But it'll be something else next time, won't it? Like it always has been. How come you're suddenly so concerned?"

Michael himself didn't know. "No, it won't be anything else, at least not from me. I'm finished

34

with all that. Maybe it taught me a lesson. That's it — taught me a lesson."

"God, you're pathetic!" Rosie eyed him. "Taught you a lesson? You dump a load of possums on *my* head and it teaches *you* a lesson? What you're saying is that in order for you to learn something, someone else has to pay the price. That's what you're saying. Talk about weak!"

Michael gritted his teeth. This was the real smart Perkins, all right. Well, no matter how smart she was, this time she wouldn't get under his skin. Rosie smiled, half to herself, half at him. She knew exactly what she was doing to him.

All of a sudden, Michael grinned. "I know what game you're playing. It's what you always do and what you've done ever since you were little. I can remember it right back to when we first started school."

"What am I doing?" she asked.

"See!" he yelled triumphantly. "You're doing it again. You know I can't — sort of — get out properly what I want to say to you. And you're taking — taking . . . what is it?"

"Advantage?"

"That's it."

"You're right," Rosie replied. "This time you're quite right and you damn well deserve it. You sure do deserve it." She smiled a small, half smile at him.

For the life of him he could not remember seeing her smile before. She just never did. "Yeah. I guess I do deserve it," he said, and risked an equally small smile at her.

"Yesterday, you and Calvin and Freddy punished me for being what I am. Or at least that's all it was to you. Now I really am being everything I am, right at you."

"Yeah, I know. I can feel it."

Rosie studied him for a moment, then said, "So what are you going to do about it? Whack me again for being smart?" And then, not really knowing why, she let him halfway off the hook. "Look, I know I get under your skin. Or, as you would put it, up your nose. I can't help that. It's just me. I can't help it anymore than you can help being irritated by it. I know you're sorry. Not so much for teaching me what you think is a lesson, but for the way you went about it."

"Dunno," said Michael. "Dunno at all."

"I know you don't. But there's one thing you should know — should understand. You must understand what you did to me. You and your two friends abused me. A gang of you against just one of me. Three of you against one person — and for no real reason at all. You lay in wait, all of you, and did something really dirty to me. Now you listen good, Michael Geraghty, by doing something like that, you took something away from me, sort of violently. And — and — and . . . there was nothing I could do to stop it. You gave me no chance to protect myself. You gave me no chance to do anything but give in to you."

Michael sat, fingers plucking at a blade of grass, eyes not meeting hers. "Yeah," was all he said.

"You know what I mean?" she asked.

36

"Yeah. Guess I do. Except you put it into words no one can understand."

She knew she had not said too much. Even if she had, she reasoned, it was no more than he deserved. "You understand, all right. Don't try to make out you don't. Biggest word I used was, I think, irritated. Even you should know the meaning of that!"

Michael risked looking at her. "It's not so much the words you use. It's what you do with them that makes it hard to work out what you mean. Like, well, what you said to me just now — I've got to think about it."

They sat for a few moments in silence, then Rosie stood to leave. Michael stood up too. "Do you have to go?" he asked.

"What's there to stay for?" she said.

"How's your possum?" he enquired.

This time she laughed. Loud and right at him. "She's all right. Why? Nowhere near big enough for you to skin. Not yet." She did not sit down again.

"Aw, I didn't mean that. Just — well — it's pretty clever to keep one, a little one, and keep it alive. It's hard to do."

"How do you know? Have you tried?" asked Rosie, interested.

"Only when I was little. Brendan — he's my brother — he gave me one he caught. But it died. Mostly they do. I think I overfed it."

"That's quite likely," commented Rosie. "You must get a lot of them when you're trapping."

37

"Yeah, quite a few."

"What do you do with them?"

"Kill them. Knock 'em on the head," he replied, simply. Rosie just looked at him. "I mean — well . . ." he started, embarrassed. "You can't just keep them. It's a fluke, your one. Most of the time it'd be cruel."

"I suppose you're right," said Rosie, and she thought of Plum.

"And I still mean what I said when I saw you find your possum. Would've been better to have put it out of its misery then. I am right, you know."

"I've got to go. I'm late." Rosie looked at Michael as if she was seeing him for the first time. There was no face jeering at her now. He was serious. Quiet and serious. Might well be as thick as a brick, she thought to herself, but he wasn't all bad.

"What I said before is true," he said, awkwardly. "I really am sorry for what I done."

"Did," she corrected him.

"For what I did," he said.

"I know you are," said Rosie and walked off up the road.

"We had her real good. Why stop now? I've worked out how we can get into her place and grab her possum. Real easy," said Cal. "Aw, come on. Why can't we?"

"We done enough," said Michael firmly.

"You gone soft," said Cal.

"So what? I gone soft then," said Michael. "It's little kids' stuff, anyway. The other was, too.

38

Whoever heard of kidnapping a possum?"

"Well, I dunno," said Fred, joining the conversation. "There was this bit on TV about a lady in the States who got two kids to kidnap a dog what'd beaten up on her dog. Then they all gave it hell."

"Hey, good one," said Cal enthusiastically. "We could get . . ."

"Cut it out," snapped Michael. "Anyone who'd get their kicks out of torturing a possum is bloody sick in my book."

He was getting a bit tired of Cal and Freddy, he thought. Not completely tired of them. Not yet. After all, they had been friends for longer than he could remember. They weren't too bad, really, not if he kept them in line. It's just that these days they seemed more sort of — well, more juvenile than himself. Pity they weren't too bright. It was impossible to have a decent conversation with either of them. Mind you, conversation with his mother was scarcely more satisfying, he thought.

"I don't care if you have rugby training eight nights a week," she told him, "as far as I'm concerned, you still have to mow the lawns. Besides, what's all this with rugby training? It's still the middle of summer!" She wrinkled her forehead at him.

"It's pre-season training. Gotta do it. Coach says . . ."

"Pre-season training be blowed, and I don't care what the coach says. If you ask me, it's ridiculous! You've only just finished the last season. You're up to something, my man — don't try pulling the wool over my eyes. Late home day in and day out.

39

Well, let me tell you — *this* coach says the lawns are to be mown. Right now and with no argument. This very minute. Before you've had something to eat."

"But my possums . . ."

"Your possums will wait. And the sooner you've finished with those smelly things the better."

"Better'n doing stupid lawns," he muttered.

"Don't you give me your lip, young man. You're not too big yet for a clip around the ears. As bad as your brothers and no mistake." She smiled. "And to think, once upon a time when you were little I thought I might have had something different in you." She ruffled his hair and gave him a kiss.

He thought he was winning. "Well, I'll just . . ."

But she outsmarted him, ". . . mow the lawns."

"Good Lord!" exclaimed his father later. "If that kid leaves any bigger border round the edge of that front lawn, we might as well give up on it altogether!"

"Mother's going away tomorrow," Mr. Perkins told Rosie at breakfast.

"Uh-huh." There was no surprise in her reaction.

"They're going to have another go at the hospital to find out what's behind her migraines."

"How long will she be away this time?"

"Two, three weeks. Don't you worry," said her father. "I know my Princess can manage."

There was, indeed, no surprise. It was by now

a yearly happening. Rosie sighed. Why hadn't her mother told her herself? Why wasn't her mother telling her anything these days? Nothing at all. "Are you taking her down?" asked Rosie.

"Yes. Be back by dinner. Now, don't you worry."

"I'm not worried, Daddy. I just wondered. What about the shop?"

"I've put a note on the door. I just won't open today. One day of the year won't hurt if they don't get their mowers done."

It was Rosie's parents' shop. It had been this business that had brought Reg Perkins to the town twenty years earlier. An engineer on one of the inter-island ferries, and already in his mid-thirties, Reg had decided to try life ashore. He chose Cooper's Junction not for the sake of the town itself — few people did that — but because it was there that he had found a business to suit him.

A country town of some two thousand people, the place existed solely as a service center for a large country area. Cooper had been an original surveyor of the land. No one knew where the Junction part of the name came from. It had never been a joining place for either rail or road.

None of which bothered Reg Perkins on his arrival in the town. Single, not unfriendly but of very few friends, he had slipped quietly into the routine of life in his shop, selling and fixing lawn mowers. He had also settled into the only boarding house in the town; a larger than usual private house that took a handful of paying guests. Indeed, the handful was just themselves and their landlady when Mr. Perkins met the future Mrs.

Perkins. Of similar age, they drifted together. Edith Saunders was a school teacher, teaching English at the local high school and disliking almost every minute of it. She found the pupils noisy, uncooperative and, in Edith's opinion, not at all interested in learning what she had to offer. Most of her students saw the place as little more than a waiting room for "life" — which would begin the moment they left school for the excitement of work in the few shops, offices and trades of the town, the local dairy factory and the outlying farms.

Meeting Reg meant escape, too, for Edith. They married, and when Edith was almost forty, Rosie was born. Two years later, Rosie's brother was born. The town was surprised. The baby boy died and it was soon after his death that Edith Perkins first became ill. She took to her bed each afternoon and did not leave it until the following morning, attending only briefly and casually to the needs of her daughter. Rosie made little demand on her mother's time.

Edith began to drink. By now she needed one bottle of sherry a day to get herself through the afternoons, evenings and nights that she spent in the dusty, shuttered bedroom where she lived most of her life. Outwardly, it would have appeared a reasonably normal existence, except to those people in a small town who always suspect the lives of those who live quietly among them.

Routines had developed over the years. Rosie and her father would leave the house each morning at eight-thirty, driving in his pick-up truck first to drop Rosie off at school and then on to his workshop. Edith would leave the house at ten, having done whatever housework was necessary. Driving her Mini she would arrive at the shop soon after and, in businesslike fashion, would deal with accounts, books and banking. Then, unless it was Friday, she would go home. On Fridays she shopped for her family — making brief visits to the supermarket and the butcher's and wherever else she thought it necessary. Once home, she went to bed and neither husband nor daughter shared her company until the following morning. Indeed, on weekends they saw nothing of her at all.

The past year had shown signs that the order of the fabric of life Edith Perkins had created was coming apart. Once, she had driven from home in the morning, become lost, and found herself hours later in another town. More recently she had lined up at the supermarket checkout, not with her groceries but clutching the business banking of the previous day. The people of the town began to take a closer interest in Mrs. Perkins' headaches.

Neither Reg nor Edith Perkins had a friend in the whole world. They, with Rosie, were a tiny island of existence complete in themselves.

"Do you think she'll get better this time?" Rosie asked her father.

"We'll see, Princess. But don't you worry your pretty little head about suchlike. You'll see, everything will be all right. You and me still got each other, you know." He took her in his arms and, very still, she accepted his embrace.

Afterwards, as Rosie fed Plum, she mimicked her father's voice, "Mother's going away tomorrow." Then, with a force that startled the animal, "God! Why can't he leave me alone! Why can't he keep his hands off me? I don't want his hands. I don't want him, I don't want him near me. Not now, not ever . . ."

The possum returned and took a piece of apple from her outstretched fingers. Absentmindedly Rosie stroked the fur on the back of Plum's neck. "Don't you worry your pretty little head about suchlike." Again a mimicking. "Mother's going away. So what? When was she ever here?" She picked up her pet which allowed itself to be held. Rosie continued to stroke the creature. "I want her, Plum. I want my mother. I want her here with me. I want to be with her and her to be with me. I do. I love her, Plum. I want her to love me and I want to help her. I think I can — I could help her."

The animal suddenly struggled from her grasp and scuttled back into its cage in a chattering of disapproval. "Possum! What the hell do you know about anything? Seems all you want is a prison. Is that what I've done to you? Are you my Princess? No. Oh, no. Not that. What then? Can't think that my meddling in your life is going to help you. Just a different sort of trap, that's all. Traps? Us Princesses get trapped, eh Plum? One way or another we get trapped and there's nothing we can ever do about it. Not really."

She shut the door of Plum's cage, then curling her fingers into the wire of the cage, spoke softly to the possum. "What does my father want from me, Plum? How does he see me? Am I still just his little girl, or am I becoming something else? Does he see me as her? As Mummy?" Plum ignored her presence completely, choosing to chitter unintelligibly at the same morsel of apple Rosie had given her five minutes before.

"Us Princesses get trapped, eh," repeated Rosie, and she shuddered.

Chapter Five

On the day her father took her mother to the hospital, Rosie met Michael again on the road.

"How about I come and see your possum?" he suggested.

"I don't think that'd be a good idea at all. Why?" She looked up suspiciously from where she sat beside him on the grassy bank.

"It's just — well — I'd like to see it, that's all. Really, I would." He smiled at her. "You can trust me."

"I doubt it. Besides, I just don't know."

"Aw, come on. You just told me your old lady and old man had gone away."

"It's not that," said Rosie, staring at the ground. She was thinking that if she took him, it would be the first time ever that she had taken a friend home. Friend? Was that what he was? She made

46

up her mind and walked off, indicating with the slightest movement of her head that he could follow.

He had passed her gate a thousand times. Ten thousand times. Maybe more. But he had never, ever been through it. A tangle of overgrown roses in late bloom springing from unweeded beds stretched forever, it seemed to Michael, in all directions, surrounding and dotting the most beautiful lawns he had ever seen. Quite simply, he had never suspected it would be like this. From the road, all that could be seen at the end of the long driveway was the roof of the house.

She read his thoughts. "Daddy does the lawns. He tries out all his mowers on our lawns — mainly the ones people bring for him to fix."

"Oh God, I wish he'd come to our place. He could try them out at our place as much as he likes," said Michael with heartfelt sincerity.

Rosie took Plum from her cage. The possum used her as she would a tree; clinging, climbing and moving in and out of her long hair. "She's happier, I think, when it's dark — nocturnal. She can talk, you know. A sort of funny chittery-chattering."

"Yeah, I know," said Michael. "Should hear them when they get . . ." He stopped short, changing direction. "Gee, she's got a choice pelt."

"Yes — and it's hers, not yours," warned Rosie.

"Gotta be honest," he said. "I wouldn't mind taking it when she's a bit bigger. None of the wear and tear they get out in the bush. Sure is choice." He softly stroked the silky fur. "Can I hold it?"

"That's up to her. Come on, Plum. Come and see your not very nice visitor. You nearly met him once before but we'll forget about that." She passed Plum to Michael who cradled the animal gently against his chest.

"What d'you feed it?" He extended a finger and Plum licked at it.

"Oh, just about anything now. Even tried her on ice cream," said Rosie. "I'm trying to get her onto the shoots of things — even shoots from the roses out there. She's not too keen."

"I'd keep it on ice cream if I was you. It's munching the tender shoots of things that gets them into real bad trouble. Give it a go on bananas. Might grow up thinking it's a monkey!"

"Look, it's *her* and *she*, not *it*. You have so much to do with them I don't suppose you ever notice."

"Can't help but notice," said Michael. He considered explaining to her the differences between skinning males and females — but somehow it didn't seem quite the right time.

Rosie put Plum back in her cage and turned to Michael. She didn't want him to go now that he was here. "Would you like something to drink?" she asked.

"Sure. What've you got?"

"Lemonade, I think . . . or maybe a cup of tea?"

"Aw, I thought you meant something else. Still, a cup of tea'd be okay." He followed Rosie into the house. Immediately he was conscious of the shut-up feeling of the place and the dank, musty smell. It was quite dark, and he noticed that all the curtains were either drawn or half drawn. His eyes slowly accustomed to the gloom. "Whew, you've got some real old things."

"I suppose they are. I don't really know but I suppose they are." Rosie had seen very few other houses and had almost nothing with which to compare the rugs, silver, old brass, furniture and pictures.

"Where'd you get it all from?"

She was uncertain. "It's always been here. I think it belonged to my grandparents — my mother's parents. They're dead. I never knew them, but I think they once lived in India."

"Well, I reckon they must've lived in a museum, if you ask me. You got a video and things?" Michael asked curiously.

"No, we haven't got a video," replied Rosie. "Nothing like that at all."

"I'm trying to convince my old man that everyone's got a video. Everyone else I know has got a video. Can't get him to see that we really need one."

"Well then, now you know two places that haven't got one."

"That's no help to me at all," said Michael.

"Well, we haven't one. We haven't got a television and we haven't got a stereo either. All we've got is a radio," said Rosie honestly.

"Whew!" commented Michael.

They made the tea together and took it out onto the long verandah that spread across the width of the house.

"This is nice," said Michael.

Rosie mistook his meaning. "It's only tea," she said.

"No — I mean all this." He indicated the wild garden and the brilliant, green, closely-mown lawns. "The tea's okay, though," he added.

"You're funny. You really are funny," said Rosie.

"Why? Why am I funny? I don't think I'm funny at all." He put down his cup and leaned back against the verandah post with his hands behind his head, waiting for her reply.

"A month ago you hated me," explained Rosie. "You really and truly loathed me. And not only for a brief time, either — it was sort of forever. You can't deny that, Michael."

"I know," he said. "I've thought about it, too, but I don't know why. Maybe it's part of growing up. Dunno. Maybe it took those dead possums for me to see you as you really are. Something like that."

"Do you realize you always give a sort of throw-away line? It's either dunno, or, something like that. Shows you're a lazy thinker."

"Or it could show that I really and truly don't know." He smiled at her. "Or something like that."

Rosie returned his smile. "You can't deny though that you disliked me very, very deeply."

"Well — a man can change," said Michael.

"You're not a man! Not yet," teased Rosie.

"Not far off it, but. Look!" He jumped to his feet and stripped off his shirt. "See? Hairs under my arms and one on my chest — and I'm fifteen soon."

50

"You're just fourteen. I know that. And it sounds as if you should keep off the bananas," Rosie joked.

"What? Anyway, I've still got the hairs. I'm — what's it called? — mature, I think it is."

"You're mad," said Rosie. "And your hairs only show because you have such a dark complexion. Very dark really." She looked at him with a degree of interest.

"I know." He sighed and settled down again. "My mum says I'm a drawback."

"You're a what?" laughed Rosie.

"Nothing to laugh about," said Michael. "A drawback. You know what I mean? Least I think that's what she said." He thought for a while. "Yeah, a drawback. We're Irish, see."

"So?"

"It's something to do with that thing of ships from Spain a long time ago. The Spains all got shipwrecked and they swam to Ireland and married nice Irish ladies — and that's why, quite often Mum says, you get Irish people like me what are drawbacks. See?"

"The Spanish Armada. Spanish not Spains. And it's throwback, not drawback, though it seems to me you're one of them, too," said Rosie.

"Jeez, you're smart. Just as well I can put up with it," Michael said.

"Well, there's no sense in letting you continue as ignorant as you are," laughed Rosie.

"Huh! Well, anyway, that's why I'm so dark."

Rosie eyed him up and down. "Has anyone ever told you you're quite good-looking?" She kept her eyes on him.

51

He blushed and Rosie laughed again. Michael blushed even more. "Whew! You sure say things like no one else ever does."

"I say what I think." She stopped smiling. "And you know damn well that's what always gets me in trouble. I don't think I could change though. Not really. I don't mean to be smart. I do think you look quite good so I say so. You've got all that curly, black hair and a nice, tanned skin and sort of bright, blue eyes. And they all go together. You must have noticed — don't you ever look in the mirror?"

"Yeah . . . but . . . I dunno. Really, I dunno." He sounded confused. Of course he knew what he looked like. Of course he could see that all the parts seemed to go together reasonably well. But you just couldn't say so about yourself!

Rosie persisted. "I'll tell you another thing . . ." she began.

"Do you have to?"

". . . when I was little, I thought you were related to the devil."

"Why?" Genuine surprise this time.

"Because of your pointed, black eyebrows. I must have seen a picture somewhere of the devil, and — well — I put two and two together, and nothing about you ever gave me any reason to think I wasn't right!"

"But I'm a good boy. Most of the time, anyway. You just never knew me — the *real* me." He paused. "Seeing as we're getting all personal, what about you then?"

"Well, *I'm* certainly not related to the devil —

what about me?" She sounded surprised.

"Ha! You don't sound so sure now it's your turn," Michael said with satisfaction. "Let's face it. Not many people I know've got green eyes. And your face looks a whole lot different when you smile. And my mum says your hair is a crowning glory and if she had ever had a daughter it would have been just her luck that she'd have turned out looking like me or my brothers," said Michael.

"I can see her point," Rosie smiled sweetly. "But anyway, your brothers don't look like you." She hoped she had got him sidetracked from his analysis of her.

"No, they don't. None of them. They're redheads, all of them."

"I think my old man, as you would call him, would say that they were even greater drawbacks than you. Morons, he used to call them."

"Why'd he do that? They're all right. They're good guys." Michael sounded indignant.

"He says the day they got bikes was the beginning of the end. After that, it was all downhill — motorbikes, guns, cars. When they all lived at home we certainly didn't need a stereo. And once one of them shot two of our chickens!"

"Aw, they did not! They wouldn't have done that." Michael defended his brothers stoutly.

"They did so. It was when I was small and I saw it. Daddy said it was a blessing every time he heard one of them had left home. They're not in prison, are they?" she asked, very sweetly.

"Hell, no. Why?"

"Well, Daddy always reckoned they would be before they were twenty."

"Of course they're not in prison. Brendan's a carpenter and so's Patrick. Sean's in the seminary." Helluva lot she knew, he thought.

"In the cemetery?"

He hooted in triumph. "Ha, ha, ha! Now I know something you don't! He's going to be a priest. You know, a minister. It takes years. He's very holy, is Sean."

"Yes," agreed Rosie. "It was Sean who shot our chickens."

"Seems you reckon we're a real bad family. Let me tell you, we're really very good. Bet *you* don't go to church all the time." Michael felt it was getting to the point where he really had to stand up and be counted on behalf of his family.

"You don't either. You only go on Sundays."

"Yeah, Possum Perkins knows it all. S'pose you just hide away in here and spy on us all the time. Let me tell you, too, if it hadn't been for my mum, we'd have all been sent away to school."

She wasn't about to let him off the hook. "That sure would've pleased my old man," she said. "Why wouldn't she let you go?"

"My mum said that over her dead body was anyone going to take her boys before she was good and ready. Seems she's not quite ready until each of us is about eighteen — and even that's a bit soon for her. She loves us, see," said Michael.

"Your mum must be a saint," commented Rosie. "Now, you'd better go — my old man's due home."

* * *

54

Michael walked home. There was less need to run these evenings. He had brought in his trap-line and all that was left for him to do, possum-wise, was to prepare his harvest of skins for sale. For a couple of months from late March on, there was no point in trapping. The mating season pro-duced damaged skins of inferior quality. The bucks fought for supremacy over their territory, and the none-too-gentle act of mating meant that the skins of the females also took a beating.

He climbed the hill above the big beech tree where he, Cal and Fred had lain in wait for Rosie. It seemed such a long time ago. He sat on the bank that rose up behind the tree and was still perched there, unseen, when Rosie's father drove swiftly by, down the middle of the road, in the dusk. All right for old Perkins to criticize his brothers — wasn't that hot a driver himself.

Michael sat there and wondered. Had his brothers been any noisier than others? They had been good. They still were good, all three of them. And all guys had motorbikes and cars. He should have told Rosie to let her old man know that his possum skins would mean a motorbike for him next year, too. The only snag was that he had yet to convince his parents.

He dreamed up a picture of himself on a Ya-maha with Rosie riding pillion, hair streaming out behind her from under her safety helmet. Well, maybe not. It'd be just like her to be riding the damn thing with him on the pillion behind her!

Michael continued thinking about Rosie, trying to make some sense of why she was suddenly there, plonk, right in the middle of his life. Such a short time ago she had been an object of absolute scorn. And yet, she was still the same person. She hadn't changed — still as smart as ever. Had he changed? No, he didn't think so. Not him. Well then, if he hadn't changed, why was it that Cal and Freddy seemed so dumb and boring these days — really boring, and everything they wanted to do was so childish? Why was it that he could hardly wait until after school every day, and the quick jog to beat Rosie to Old Dump Road?

Rosie sure knew a lot and was good to talk to. She could talk about almost anything. More than likely she spent all her time reading. Not that there was much option at her home — no telly, no video. Just her old man and old lady and who'd ever want to talk to them? And now her old lady was in the hospital for headaches. Huh! Not what he had heard. Everyone knew Ma Perkins got her headaches from a bottle.

When you looked closely at her, Rosie surely looked good. Yet, unlike most of the other girls he knew, she didn't seem to know it. If she did know, it didn't seem to make any difference to her. She was so beautiful with that hair and her quiet, quiet face and strange, green eyes. Almost as beautiful, he thought, as his mother's picture of the Blessed Virgin with the bleeding heart. A wonderful work of art, that — and just like Rosie. Mind you, there was no indication that the Virgin's eyes were green, her hair certainly wasn't blonde, and she did have a round face, whereas

Rosie's was rather long and thin. Still, they were both very lovely.

"I would have thought, Michael, that now you've finished with your possums we just might see you at home slightly more often. Your father and I are quite forgetting what you look like."

"Pre-season training," he muttered and speared a piece of cold meat.

"Well," said his father slowly, "I was talking to Ron Jackson today, and he was telling me . . ." He caught his son's eye and continued with a knowing half smile. "Well, he was saying something about it, anyway."

"Training or whatever, doesn't get the lawns mown or tidy your room. The good Lord knows I gave up on your brothers, but yours is even worse than theirs used to be."

"I done it, Mum. Really," Michael protested.

"Did it, not done it. And you didn't. If you thought you did, maybe you were actually working in the room next door. Do you know, I found a sweater under your bed today that I'd forgotten you even owned!"

"I'll do it tomorrow, Mum. Lawns, too. I will — really — I will."

"You'd better," said Mrs. Geraghty.

"Mum," he began, "er . . ."

"Er what?"

"Well, er . . ." He didn't quite know how to start but finally summoned up the courage and waded on in. "Would it be all right if I asked someone to lunch or dinner, maybe, on the weekend?"

"What's all this about, Michael?" his mother asked. "To be honest, you don't usually ask until you've got them here and I'm about to dish up! Put it this way, if it's Calvin and Fred, I've told you before that I'll have one or the other of them but not both. Definitely not both." Mrs. Geraghty pulled a face. "The last time . . ."

"No, it's not Cal or Fred," he said, wishing he had never asked. He knew he was sweating — it was so damn hot in this room.

"Well, who then, dear?" asked his mother with surprise.

Mr. Geraghty kept his eyes directly on his son, saying nothing but smiling the other half of the smile he had used a few moments before.

"It's — well, it's — well — Rosie. Rosie Perkins. You know her, they live just up the road." His heart beat too hard and he was sure they could see it thumping.

"Of course I know Rosie Perkins, dear. But you'll forgive me if I sound more than a little surprised. I don't think I've ever heard you say a good word about the poor little thing. Never! And when you were both at kindy . . ." She smiled at him as he started to gather up their dinner plates. "My word! Yes, of course you may invite her. Rosie Perkins! My goodness me!"

Mr. Geraghty continued looking at his son. This time he collected both halves of his smile and grinned at Michael. "Pre-season training, eh?"

* * *

It happened in math, right at the end of the period. It was a dull, hot afternoon in late March — thunder weather. The last period of the day. Most of the class were hot, tired and very, very bored. Receiving the results of a mid-term math test proved to be the last straw. With one exception, all had failed to reach even the halfway mark, and the mumbles of discontent grew as the list was read in a dead flat voice by Mrs. Pratt, their teacher. She punctuated the list of scores with comments on their abilities (particularly their lack of), their general progress (again a lack), the absence of any intelligence in the group and, if all else failed, their personal appearance.

"Clark, John, twenty-three. Wasn't it only last week you told us computer science was to be lucky enough to secure your services? Ford, Albert, eighteen; yes, well. Geraghty, Michael, thirty-one; what a pity you're not more like your brothers. Kingi, Paula, forty-five; there could be hope for you yet, Missy. Lester, Gabrielle, twenty-six; tch, tch, tch — less time on the old hair and fingernails might see an improvement there, though I have my doubts. Simple addition is about all I've come to expect from you. Newman, Calvin, seven; somewhere up on high when they were doling out brains, Calvin, the good Lord looked the wrong way when you were held out. Perkins, Rosa, eighty-seven; a bright and shining example to us all, Rosie." Mrs. Pratt's smile became genuine for the first time. "Why is it, my dear, that none of your little chums can take a leaf from your book? Why?"

Rosie sat passive, unmoving. She hoped and

prayed that the woman's holding her up as an example might soon be forgotten — overlooked by the end of the period — and that in their haste to quit the place her peers would ignore her. She showed no reaction to the praise. Let nothing show in her manner that might inflame the others. This, she knew full well, was not always enough.

Rosie slipped quickly from the room as soon as the teacher released them but she was not quite quick enough to avoid retribution just beyond the front gate. A group of them were already waiting. Accident or design? It didn't really matter — they were there and formed a gauntlet that had to be run. All were in fine form for a round or two with Rosie.

"Jeez, you get up my nose . . ."

"Get up my everything!"

"Smart bitch, Perkins . . ."

"Possum Perkins, Possum Perkins . . ."

"Time we got real even with you . . ."

Rosie tried first to push through the group, then tried to work her way around them. She could do neither. She was trapped.

"Think you know it all, don't you, Perkins?"

"If you're so smart, why don't you . . ."

"Stuff you, mole . . ."

"Possum Perkins! Mole Perkins!" They started to jostle her and move about her in a circle of menace. Rosie was used to it. She knew that if she did nothing it would end. It always did. Their anger was on the surface and, as quickly as it rose, so, too, would it evaporate. Years ago, when she was eight, ten, even twelve, the attack would have turned physical. Now, while this was still possible, it was less likely. She knew she just had to ride it out. Ride out the storm.

The language became coarser, tougher. The words meant nothing to her. She had heard them all before and they in themselves held no terror. The spite and the anger were already ebbing when Michael Geraghty came around the corner and caught the tail end of it all.

"Look any better and you'd still look worse than the backside of a cow!" Laugh, laugh.

"Or the bum of a horse with a white tail hanging down." Louder laugh.

"Mole Perkins! Slag!"

Michael stopped in his tracks. He had no difficulty at all in recognizing what was happening — so often he had been part of it himself. "Say that again?" he yelled into the face of the one who had flung the last insult. The others, only four or five stayers now, started at the unexpected tone of his voice. Some, in the process of drifting away, sniffed the scent of something new, a drift to a new direction. They stopped, turned and hurried back. "Say what you said, again!" Michael yelled, louder.

The boy, often a friend and generally an ally, was puzzled. "She's a slag. Old Mole Perkins . . ." He got no further. Michael clenched his fist and hit hard. Below the belt. His target doubled over, winded, the pain on his face not quite rubbing out the look of surprise. However, this, too, was wiped from his eyes as Michael followed through with a knee to the groin. Now he crumpled com-

61

pletely. The eyes of the others darted in all directions. There was no sound at all other than a hoarse rasping and gasping from the ground.

Michael took Rosie's arm. She resisted his touch and his hand fell to his side. The two of them moved off. To the spectators, it appeared that they walked off closely, quickly and together. Around the town center, across the bridge and down into Old Dump Road; they didn't speak. They reached the tree.

"Sit down," he yelled at her, ordering. She kept on walking. "Hey!" he called after her. "Hey!" Louder. "Hey, Rosie!"

She turned. Her face was as furious and almost as contorted as it had been on that other day in almost the same place. "Don't you ever do that to me again, do you hear me? Never. Do you understand?"

Shock showed on Michael's face. "What the hell . . . ?" Rosie calmed enough to sense, then recognize, his surprise. She took a fitful step, then two, back toward him. He moved toward her, rubbing a hand across his forehead. Bewildered. "What did I do, Rosie? What did I do?"

"Oh God," moaned Rosie. "Oh God, you don't know, do you? You really don't know." She sat down and pulled him down to sit beside her. "How can I make you understand? Why in hell didn't you stick to throwing dead possums at me? God, it was easier then. Now . . . ?"

He sensed her tone of despair and recognized that it was mixed with anger. "I dunno," was all he could say. The despair he felt was the equal of hers. "For God's sake, tell me what I done?"

"Did. Okay. First — never, ever physically attack anyone on my account. I don't need it, I never have. You've got enough brain," she smiled slightly at him, "a whole thirty-one percent of it, to know that. What you butted in on before is just, quite simply, part of my life. Just a part of what happens to me, as you know damn well. I don't pretend that I like it, nobody would. But I can tolerate it. It doesn't even happen as often or as badly now as it once did. Do you understand, Michael?" She had spoken slowly, seriously.

"Dunno." He rolled facedown on the grass and his voice was muffled. "I suppose I do know what you're saying."

"I can't really expect you to understand — you've always been on the other side. And to me, Michael, for a helluva long time, you *were* the other side. You were really, really nasty, and I guess I still find it hard to believe that leopards change their spots or that new leaves get turned over."

"What?"

"I don't need you to fight my battles, Michael. I can fight my own. And please, don't use physical force on my behalf. I don't believe in it — not ever. You'd probably never realize in a month of Sundays that I was actually winning that one back there. Two, three minutes more and they would all have gone."

"So I done the wrong thing." He turned away from her so she couldn't see his face. Classic, he thought to himself, real classic. Guts and nuts in ten seconds flat. Whew! She couldn't expect him

63

to turn into a saint overnight. "I sure got him one though, didn't I? He sure knew something had hit him for what he done." He turned back to her, hopefully.

She ignored his last comments. "I've only said the easy bit."

"You mean there's more?" He pulled a face.

"Of course there's more. What I'm telling you is that there's more to life than math scores," she said.

"You don't have to tell me that — I know," said Michael.

"Yes. Well, there's more than a few of my little chums, as old Pratt calls them, who are interested in a damn sight more than your brain," said Rosie, looking sideways at him. "Heard three or four of them in the bathroom only last week, and it wasn't your brain they were discussing. What were they calling you?"

Michael was puzzled. "Well, I dunno, do I? I could hardly've been there with them!"

"Chunk? No, that's not it . . . monk? Doubt it. Mind you, what with a brother in the cemetery . . ." He knew she was laughing at him but he didn't mind. "Well, I might be rather thick on things that aren't math and science but even *I* knew what they were getting at. Spunk? Hunk? One of those. I don't precisely know what they meant — maybe you do?"

A small smile spread across his face and then disappeared. "Nothing much we can do about that, is there?" Something told him he should be feeling better about it than he did. "So what? It's a load of crap, anyway."

"Reckon it is at that," said Rosie, smiling at him. "But it's one other thing I'm going to have to live with."

"And I'm not allowed to smash their faces in if they say or do anything, right?"

"Right. Michael, I've got to go now, I'm late. I can't thank you for what you did, you know that. But I can thank you for thinking of me."

"Reckon I'll never know with you," he said. He was quiet for a moment, then smiled. "What you mean is that I done the wrong thing but for the right reason."

"Yep," agreed Rosie, "you done the wrong thing." She turned to him and, without warning, kissed him very softly on the cheek. Then she was away, running, her hair streaming behind her into the tunnel of trees. He sat for a moment and his fingers touched the place on his cheek where he could still feel the touch of her lips. He wandered home, wondering.

Rosie, too, wondered. "You show as much sign of turning into a monkey as I do, Plum. Or as he does. Have another slice." She poked another piece of banana through the wire of the cage into Plum's outstretched paw. Then she took the possum from the cage and sat with her on the floor of the shed while Plum snuffled at the fruit smell on her hands. Rosie drew her knees up to her chest and smiled, as much to herself as at her pet. "He fought for me, Plum. That's what he did. He did it for me."

She closed her eyes and stroked Plum's fur, still smiling. "No matter how wrong it was — and it was wrong — he did it for me. And I yelled at him because it was wrong. Violence is wrong, Plum, absolutely wrong." She sighed. "I don't know how to work it out — how to equate it. All I know is," she said as she picked the possum up and got to her feet, "I like him very much indeed. I . . . I like him — like him a lot." Rosie spoke with some force as she put Plum in her cage and closed the door. She extended her finger through the wire for the creature to suck. "It's true, Plum — I do."

Chapter Six

"You've a lovely name, Rosie," commented Mrs. Geraghty. "How did you get it? Is it your mother's name?" It showed how little she knew about her only near neighbours, she thought to herself.

"It's not actually Rosie at all," replied Rosie, "it's Rosa."

"Rosa! What a handle!" hooted Michael.

"Be quiet, Michael," scolded his mother.

"It's Rosa Dorothy Perkins," continued Rosie.

"Yeah, I knew that. Sometimes they call out your whole name at school."

"Quiet, Michael," said his mother. "How did you come to be called that, Rosie?"

"My mother loved roses. She still does."

"I heard she was unwell . . ." said Mrs. Geraghty, enquiringly. Michael raised his eyebrows — that wasn't always the way his mother put it.

"She's much better now, thank you. Actually, she's coming home today," said Rosie. "Anyway, Dorothy Perkins is an old, old rose. We've got it at home. And Rosa, the word, is just the generic name for the plant."

Mrs. Geraghty looked at Rosie and then at her son. She wondered what possible sort of conversation the one could carry on with the other.

"You've got a lovely home, Mrs. Geraghty," said Rosie and meant every word. She could count on one hand the number of homes she had ever been invited to visit. This one, she thought, was the nicest she had ever seen. What Rosie saw was that it was light and airy, bright with color and cheerful with comfort. What she did not see, nor look for, were the very many signs that it was a well-used, rather battered and somewhat shabby home where a handful of growing sons had helped with the wearing.

Rosie felt comfortable.

Michael felt delighted.

Mr. and Mrs. Geraghty felt strange.

Rosie had not lied to her father. She had told him truthfully that she did not want to go with him to collect her mother. That she had more than a small pile of homework to get through was also absolutely true. That she was more used to staying home to prepare dinner was undoubtedly fact. There had been no need to add that she was about to go off on her first lunch date ever!

68

"How do you think Mummy will be this time?" she had asked.

"Don't you worry your pretty head, Princess. Your mother'll be fine," her father had answered.

Yes, thought Rosie. For a few weeks everything would be fine. After that, the year was likely to run its usual course. Somehow, these days, things seemed to get worse more quickly during the periods in between her mother's stays in hospital. Rosie knew there was little she could do to help. For a month or so after coming home, she may be able to talk to her mother. Not that talking between the two of them had ever been easy. But for a few weeks at least, there was a slight chance that anything said between them just might be remembered from one day to the next. Now, after so many years of estrangement, there seemed to be so little they could talk about. So little that needed to be talked about. Was there any point, Rosie asked herself, in putting everything into one month when it seemed doomed to shrivel up and die over the following ten or eleven? This time, she thought, this time it just might be different. Please, God, let it be different. Let her be able to get through to her mother. Please . . .

Rosie looked around her in the Geraghty home. It could not have been more different from her own. She well knew that not all homes were like this any more than all homes were like her own.

"Have you thought, Rosie, of what you want to do when you leave school?" asked Mr. Geraghty, struggling to make conversation.

69

"Well, math and science are what really interest me, Mr. Geraghty," said Rosie. "I think I might go on after high school to the university. I think I'll do science."

"She's real bright," said Michael. "Got an excellent brain."

"We know that, Michael, you've been telling us for years — one way or another," said Mrs. Geraghty. "A pity you haven't taken a leaf out of Rosie's book."

"I do have to work," Rosie added very quickly. "I work very hard indeed."

"Yes," said Mr. Geraghty, "that's the secret — more work, fewer possums, less sport and so on, and someone else I know might end up as something more than a possum trapper. Now he tells us he only got forty-one in his latest math test! Honestly, I don't know what we're going to do with him."

Michael blushed and broke in very, very quickly, "Well, I've got ideas, you know, and I'm not going to end up as no possum trapper — so!"

"You'll have to get him to show you his possum skins, if you're interested, Rosie," said Mr. Geraghty. "He's got a good lot this year. Probably the best possum hunter of all our boys, eh, Mother?"

Michael struggled to change the direction of the conversation. All sitting round discussing how good he wasn't was not his idea of fun! It was never like this if Cal and Freddy came for a meal. "Yeah, I'll show her the skins," he muttered, "and then we'll . . ."

Rosie interrupted. "From what Michael's told

me, it sounds like a lot of hard work and not very nice at all. What worries me is the kind of trap he uses. I think they're inhumane."

"Well, I don't know that there *is* a humane way — a really humane way — of ever trapping a wild creature," said Mr. Geraghty. "I don't mind him using them — all our boys have used them. They're cheap and they do the job."

"What I think Rosie means is that she doesn't like the idea of animals being caught and killed," said Mrs. Geraghty.

"No, no — it's not that at all, Mrs. Geraghty. I know they're a real pest. I remember when Mummy was really into growing her roses. The possums were dreadful then and Daddy just had to do something about them. He used to shoot them. It's gin traps I don't like."

"You never said anything to me about them," said Michael, feeling rather hurt and even less pleased at the turn in conversation.

"Was there much point?" asked Rosie.

"Well, I look at it this way," he said, "there's too many of them — possums, I mean — and they do a helluva lot of damage to trees and things. They've got good fur that sells well and my dad'd half kill me if I didn't check my traps every morning." He hoped that would be the end of it. It wasn't.

"But don't you think it's wrong, Mrs. Geraghty? Gin traps?" asked Rosie.

"Honestly, dear, I can't say I've ever given it much thought. It's always been a thing between the boys and their father. I just leave it at that.

71

Perhaps it's something I should have thought of, however, when I had the whole four of them at home — and that wasn't so long ago — it'd be all I could manage to trap one of them long enough to chop the kindling or bring in the firewood. I think I could have done with a gin trap myself back then!" She smiled at Rosie. "I used to count my week a success if I managed to get them all home together on a Sunday morning with clean clothes and clean knees, ready for Mass."

After lunch, and with the matter of gin traps still not settled, Michael showed Rosie around. "You'd better see my skins," he grumbled. "Seeing as how that was about the only thing anyone talked about at lunch. That and my dumbness!"

His shed was clear; all signs of the possum season cleaned away. The dry but uncured skins crackled to her touch as Rosie stroked the soft grey and red-brown furs. He had sorted them into colors and strung them accordingly. The fur had been wire-brushed and it took a leap of the imagination to see them as they had been; alive and of the wild.

"They're lovely," said Rosie. She tried not to see her Plum similarly strung. "What happens to them now?"

"I was waiting for the buyer that comes through town but Dad's found this other place that gives a good deal and I'm sending them off next week. There's nearly seventy of them there," he said with considerable pride, "and a helluva lot of hard work."

"What'll happen to them then, when you've sold them?" asked Rosie.

"Dunno quite. Might end up in a fur auction, or it might be that this place Dad's got is the fur buyer for a fur coat firm somewhere. I think that's what it might be. Then I think they go to the States."

Rosie stroked a fur. "Just think," she said to the pelt, "someone, somewhere — anywhere — is going to wear you . . . and they don't even know it yet. They won't know where you came from. They won't even know what you looked like."

"Aw, come on. You could say that to a little lamb, eh?" He laughed at her. "Someone, somewhere, is going to eat you. Baa. And they won't even know what you looked like. Come on, let's go. You got to meet Hitler, my cat — he's real mean. Meaner'n me!"

"That's hard to imagine," said Rosie. She was happy to comply; she felt uneasy in the shed. "I don't think I could ever make you understand that it can be hard to balance reason. Sometimes, what we think and what we do are two different things. There's more to it than that, I know. Still, I just couldn't get you to understand it."

"Is that right, smart Perkins? Is that right?" Michael looked directly at her. "Why is it then, that I'm here with you today? Why is it that you're here with me? Seems to me there's no balance of reason there. Right?"

Rosie played with Plum when she got home. She took the possum from the cage and allowed her to range the verandah and fossick among the wilderness of rosebushes and shrubs that bordered the lawn. She no longer feared that the animal would escape. Always, Plum came back to her. Indeed, every brief scamper and sampling of leaf and flower would be punctuated by a return to Rosie. Almost as if the possum wanted to check that the girl was still there.

"Think I might have met half your family today, Plum. Dead flat lot they were, too. . . . Wonder how long I'm going to be able to keep you, Plum? Plum, Plum, Plum, Plum . . ." It did seem to Rosie that Plum now answered the call of her name. If repeated over and over, just occasionally it seemed as if the possum responded.

"Plum, Plum, Plum . . . They've got a really nice house, Plum. I think you would like them — Mr. and Mrs. Geraghty, that is. Mrs. Geraghty talks a lot. I would think that she's always talked a lot to her family — to her children. A very kind lady, I would think. Mr. Geraghty — well, he's a bit different. Much quieter than his wife but a kindly gentleman, I feel sure. You can just tell, Plum, that Michael is so lucky to have such loving parents. He tells me Mr. Geraghty has something to do with roads. He looks after them. I wonder what you have to do to make it a full-time job looking after roads?

"Now, their son, Michael — my friend, Michael — he's quite a different matter. You did meet him once, Plum. Actually, you've met him twice. Once, when I found you, then again when he called in here. And I really must advise you, dear

74

Plum, Plum, Plum, to treat him with the utmost circumspection and care. Circumspection. What a very good word that is. Circumspection." She rolled the word on her tongue, relished it. "He is — Michael is — quite simply rather too direct with people of your kind. People? Well, you're a person to me in most ways. Now, I'm not trying to say that Michael would deliberately hurt you as a person — I don't think he's like that — but, sadly, Plum, Plum, Plum, the end result would be very much the same for you. A health hazard to possums, is Michael. . . .

"How can it be, Plum, that someone so beautiful — and he is beautiful to me — can be so insensitive? So hard. If I asked him that, he'd just say I dunno. Well, I dunno, really, I dunno. Yet you can see his softness with that truly, truly ugly, old cat of his. Hitler. And, Plum, he's soft with me."

Her thoughts changed direction. "I wonder how she'll be this time? I wonder if it's any use? Do you think she'll talk to me for a week or two this time? You don't know, do you, Plum? You're never even seen her. It's not migraines, Plum — I don't know if it ever was. It's the booze. Seems to me, he's letting her do it to herself and I don't know why. I don't know, Plum. But I do know what it's doing to her, I do know that. It's going for her brain and it's killing her liver. I know that from a book. Funny, isn't it? Books often say what will happen — but they don't often say why. She'll die, Plum. Might take a little while yet, but sure enough she'll die. Before I've even got to know her." The possum played on in the growing shadows of the verandah, returning frequently to Rosie.

"They've got a really lovely house, Plum. Dreadful lawns, though. Truly dreadful lawns but a lovely house. Let me tell you, I'd rather have a lovely house than lovely lawns, any day! It's warm, their house. And d'you know, they talk? I bet they talk all the time. I bet they talk when Michael comes home from school and when Mr. Geraghty gets in from his roads. I wonder what he does with the roads? Never done anything on our one. They just talk. They're a sort of talking lot of people. Noisy, too. Even Mrs. Geraghty is a bit noisy. I s'pose she has to be. She's sort of a real mother. Bet she's always been with them — part of them. Not . . . not hidden away, hiding from them all. Bet it's noisy when his brothers are home — except for the one who's always praying because he's so holy. He must have quieted down a lot, that one. We know it's noisy when they all come home, Plum. You can hear them from here when the wind's blowing this way.

"Surprises me, Plum, that all that talking hasn't made Michael a little bit brighter. He's real thick to talk to sometimes, Plum. I don't know what I see in him, really. It's sure not his brain. Of course I do have hopes that he is, as they say, hiding his brain under a bushel, sort of. Michael! Michael, Michael, Michael . . ."

The possum responded to the call.

"I don't know what on earth Rosie sees in you, Michael, really I don't. She is so — well —

clever," said Mrs. Geraghty later that day.

"Meaning I'm not?" said her son. Entertaining Rosie to lunch now seemed to have been a mixed blessing.

"Silly," she said, ruffling his hair. "I didn't mean that at all. And Dad and I really are pleased with your forty-one percent in math."

"Yeah, well, I'm just no great genius, that's all." A thought struck him and he brightened cheekily. "Still, look at it this way, Mum — it's my body they're all after, not my brain."

"You can cut that out," said Mrs. Geraghty. "Body indeed!"

"She's okay, isn't she? Rosie, I mean."

"How do you mean, dear?"

"It's really quite strange how I never got to know her before."

"Seems to me you never gave her a chance before," said his mother. "She's the same Rosie now as she was this time last year, when I'm quite sure that had she asked you the time of day you'd have clocked her one!"

"That's only part of it, Mum. See, I never really knew her. I never knew she could be good to be with and good to talk to," explained Michael.

"All I can say is I'm delighted you finally did get to know her. She's a sweet girl, a nice girl . . . but not a very happy one, I suspect."

"She's worried about her mother," said Michael.

"Mmmm."

"They've got this real neat house. You should

see it, Mum. It's like a museum. Except they haven't got a telly."

"Not many museums do have a telly, dear," said Mrs. Geraghty.

"They haven't got a video, either."

"Neither have we, dear."

Michael sighed. "Yeah, well, that's one of the great tragedies of my life. I reckon them — the Perkins — and us must be the only families anywhere without one."

"Yes, dear."

"We're under — under — under something. Underdone?"

"If you say so, dear, although I think you might mean underprivileged. Or perhaps hard done by." Mrs. Geraghty closed the oven door on a batch of scones. "And just to prove it, dear, you get your hands in the sink and get those dishes done. After you've done that you can take your wonderful body and heave a few loads of wood indoors. There just might be a frost tonight."

Chapter Seven

"Your mother's tired, Princess. She's in bed now. You can see her in the morning. Now, how did my girl fill in her day?" He moved toward her. "Feeling all right now?"

Rosie moved around the table. "How is she?" She ignored her father's questions.

"Good as new again, or so they say. New course of treatment this time. Should be as right as rain, they told me."

"They" had said something similar every year for as long as Rosie could remember. She watched as her father took her mother's luggage from the utility. She saw him take several cartons from the tray of the vehicle and heard the clink of bottles as he stacked them away in what had once been the pantry. Nothing had changed. Rosie knew nothing would change. The seeds of the next harvest were well and truly planted in those boxes in the pantry. Why did he do it? Why did she, her mother, let it be done? There must be an answer somewhere.

No answer was forthcoming when Rosie took a cup of tea to her mother the next morning. The woman looking at her from the bed was both alien and familiar. Almost every day of her life Rosie had spoken words to this woman and had heard the woman speak to her. She had been cared for by this woman from birth. "Here's your tea, Mummy," she said as she placed the cup and saucer within reach of her mother.

"Thank you, Rosa. Please pass me my bag. I want my book."

"How are you feeling?"

"Very good, dear. Really very good. Now hand me my bag, would you please?"

Rosie picked up the bag and gave it to her mother. "What did they do?"

Edith Perkins looked surprised. "The usual things, Rosa, the usual things. Much better now. Now you run along and I'll get up soon."

Absolutely flatly and with no expression in her voice, Rosie said, "I want to talk to you, Mummy." Having said as much she did not know what she was going to say.

The woman put down her book and looked at her daughter. "Is something wrong, Rosa? Are you all right?"

"I — I just want to talk to you, that's all."

"Can't it wait? Are you sure everything's all right?

It's not your period, is it? Something wrong?" She sounded a touch impatient.

"No, it's not that. There's nothing wrong like that at all. I just want to talk to you. I want to talk to you about you," said Rosie a little nervously.

"About *me*, my dear? For goodness' sake, why? Look, Rosa, Mummy's tired. It's been a very hard two weeks. Now you just run along, there's a good girl." But something in her daughter's face told Edith Perkins that this was not about to happen. She sighed. "Very well then, child. You want to talk? Sit down and talk."

"We never talk," said Rosie, "not about anything." She sat, silent.

"Don't we, dear? I don't know. Of course we talk — if there's anything you want. And, of course, there's your father."

"I don't want to talk to Daddy, I want to talk to you." Rosie leaned against the back of the small bedroom chair. Clever, clever Rosie Perkins, she thought to herself; wants to talk, doesn't know what to talk about. Talk about Michael? I kissed a boy on the cheek, Mummy. Talk about Daddy? Daddy, who holds me too tight, who keeps you here in bed. About a half grown possum who's starting to mean more to me than you in your bed? Talk?

Then the words came. "Yes, Mummy, I do want to talk to you. Look at me — I'm nearly fifteen. I'm too old for you to play tricks on anymore without expecting some questions from me about what it's all about."

81

"Rosa!" her mother snapped. "About what it's all about? What are you talking about, child? Tell me what you want. What is all this nonsense?"

"It's about everything, Mummy. I want to know why you are like this. I want to know why you tell me you have sick headaches that put you to bed because they're so bad — and have put you to bed nearly every day for as long as I can remember."

"Rosa!"

Rosie did not stop. "I don't think you're sick at all. Not in a really sick way. I think you make yourself sick by drinking but what I don't know is why you do that." She stopped now, horrified by what she had managed to say and not knowing what reaction to expect. She closed her eyes and waited for what was to come. When she finally dared look at her mother, she saw with surprise that her words had had little effect. Her mother stared straight ahead, her only movement being a small, nervous tic in her eyelid.

Rosie stood. "Mummy, I'm sorry. I'll go now." She moved toward the door.

"Sit down, Rosa. Sit down again." Edith's voice was soft. She pulled herself up in bed. "I never thought it was important. It didn't seem to matter. I didn't realize it mattered to you."

"Mummy, until I knew just a little of what it was all about, I don't think it did matter. I just sort of accepted what was. I don't know when I knew," said Rosie. "But surely, it must matter to you?"

"Not really," replied her mother. "Not really."

"That can't be right, Mummy, it just can't be.

82

If it doesn't matter, then why do you go away every year?"

Her mother was silent for a minute, then spoke quietly. "It's too much to explain. It's too much to tell you just now. If you do want to know all about it, I will tell you. Not now, though. Maybe sometime soon."

"I do want to know," said Rosie.

"Very well then, Rosa. But not now."

"When?" her daughter persisted.

Edith sighed. "Why is it so important?"

Time was a factor, and Rosie knew this. But there was no way she could tell her mother that if they didn't talk together soon, very soon — in two, three weeks at most — then once again the cloud would come down on her mother's mind for another year. "You are my mother," she said, slowly. "Of course it is important to me."

"Funny little thing," Edith remarked, and smiled briefly at her for the first time. "You always were a funny little thing. An independent little person. Always were. I imagine you still are. Really, though, I can't see that any of it should matter to you — two, three years and you'll be gone. Out on your own, making your own way. Taking your own hurdles in whatever sort of stride you develop."

Hurdles were not just for when you left school, thought Rosie. She picked her words carefully. "You are my mother. You were my mother when I was born and before that even. You were my mother when I was little. You are now. You will still be my mother when I leave home and when I'm grown-up."

83

"You are a funny thing, I'm right about that," her mother repeated. "Now, if you will let me, I'd like to get up. You may run a bath for me, please. Then I have two weeks of your father's books to do. Also, I suddenly feel as if I want to have a go at the roses along the front of the house. I noticed them when I came in last night. Away for a week or two and the weeds take over entirely. You'd think your father . . ."

Edith Perkins' roses had not been touched for almost a year. Many, indeed most, had received little or no attention for even longer.

Rosie ran the hot water into the bath first and allowed herself to be enveloped into the clouds of warm steam. What hope was there, she thought, that this time she might find the key to the person who was her mother? Even then, would she be able to unlock whatever lock, whatever door it was that existed between the two of them? She prepared the bath and the bathroom and then called her mother.

Rosie fed her possum. For once there was nothing she wanted to say to the animal.

"We gotta stop meeting like this," Michael said to Rosie.

"That's up to you," said Rosie. "Found someone else, have you?"

"Course not. It's just that, well, I've really got to get down to serious training. Old Jackson — he's our coach — well, he reckons I've got a real chance of making the first fifteen. Says I'm a natural." Michael swaggered a little.

84

"That's nice for you . . . if you like that sort of thing," she said.

"You've really got no idea of what that means, have you? No idea of what a great honor it is."

"It's only a game," said Rosie. "I don't like games."

"So I'd noticed. But it's not only a game — it's a religion."

"Bet you don't tell that one to your brother in the cemetery." Rosie smiled.

"Well, I think he probably said the same thing when he was at school. And it is an honor, too. I mean to say — I'm only in the fourth form. Most of the guys on the team are in the sixth or seventh form! I'd be the youngest. Whew!" The thought overwhelmed him. "And I only just turned fourteen, too."

"Seems to me I can remember you showing me the one hair on your chest and telling me you were nearly fifteen!" said Rosie.

"Yeah, well, that was then. This is now," said Michael.

"I guess you must be quite good," she conceded.

"Good! I'm brilliant. Best fly half they've ever had, I heard someone say. We all gotta be good at something — least, that's what I reckon. With you it's all brain, cramming and learning; with me it's all physical."

"You talk absolute rubbish, Michael, and you know it," said Rosie. "With you, it could be both. You put on a big act about being dumb but you don't fool me. What's the point? What're you trying to prove? To whom are you trying to prove it?

85

You may not have the best mind in the country, but you know and I know that most of what you say is one big act!"

"Well, the other guys . . ."

"I give up," said Rosie. "I can just guess what you're going to say about the other guys."

"No, you can't, you're not a mind reader. Well, not yet," said Michael.

"It's something called peer pressure. It means that something in you won't let you appear to be brighter, better or different from all the rest — the herd, the mob. Except, that is, in those sorts of things that the herd and the gang and the mob consider are okay. Like your precious rugby. And I do know you're clever enough to know what I'm talking about. For some reason it is important to you to make yourself look and sound as thick as a fence post. Just so's you're no different from them. Do you realize it wouldn't really matter to me at all if you *were* slow and found things pretty hard at school? But you're not — you're just a big, fat fraud."

Michael looked at her. "You might be right, you might be wrong . . . but I'm not fat!"

"I couldn't care less if you were," said Rosie. "So when do these big training sessions start?"

"Next week, I think. It's only two nights a week."

"That's a relief. I didn't know how I'd make it through the week without seeing you," said Rosie.

"I think you mean that," said Michael, delighted.

"Oh, I do. I do," said Rosie as she walked off home.

* * *

He lay on his bed that night and thought of her. Should he toss in the rugby and spend the time with her? For the sake of his mind? Don't be stupid! He couldn't do that . . . could he?

It had been months now, yet it still seemed to him that she needed him no more than when they first met. Why should she, anyway? Was there any reason for her to need him? Maybe she was some sort of a witch — she'd cast a spell on him. Nothing funny about that. Once upon a time people might have thought just that. What was she? Just a strange girl. A strange, beautiful girl with a pet possum.

Michael moved restlessly at the thought of Rosie. He tried thinking about his football but the thoughts would not stick. His thoughts kept coming back to her. He wanted, needed, to see more of her. Wanted to be with her more, spend more time with her than seemed possible at present.

Friendship? Well, there was Freddy, Cal and all the others. They were his friends — better friends, too, than she was. They never argued with him, never disagreed with him, never laughed at him. They were real good friends. They always went along with him. She — Rosie — never did. Well, certainly not very often.

Cal and Fred? They were sure looking sideways at him these days. The whole school thing was funny. For a day or two after his defense of Rosie there had been eyes going this way and that. Nothing said. It was very hard to know what to do. Should he sit with her? Walk with her? Ignore

her? That she had come in for more than a little
attention from the other girls since that day, he
also knew. Rosie had told him. It had not worried
her, and in fact was probably less than she had
come to expect over the years.

Sometimes he did sit with her or near her in
class. Once or twice he sat by her at lunch. Not
that it meant much; her nose was generally stuck
in a book. There was little desire on her part for
his attention. She seemed quite unconcerned when
he went off with others.

Now she was convinced he wasn't dumb. So
what? Did it really matter? Maybe it was time to
give it a burst and do slightly more than the bare
minimum of work. What was it about her that
held him? Her eyes? Green, clear and direct.
Honest. Just one look from them let you know
when she thought you were talking a load of bull.

He lay there and pondered; worried over why
she should be so unpopular. If he could see her
for what she was, why couldn't the others? Kids
with a brain could be popular, too, so it couldn't
just be that. Maybe, then, it was her manner; the
way she indicated quite clearly that she needed
none of them. She was herself to herself, her own
person. She had little interest in what they said,
little interest in what they did.

Yet Rosie cared for him. Didn't she? Hadn't she
shown that she cared for him? Michael tossed
more restlessly and suddenly the room seemed
unbearably hot. He got up, opened the window
and stared into the night in the direction of the
Perkins' house. What would she be doing now?

Bloody fool question — she'd be asleep.

"You're a bloody fool, Michael Geraghty," he spoke softly to himself. "Whatsit they say? You need a cold shower. A freezing shower, actually. That or a hard game of rugby. Perhaps that's what showers and rugby are for. Something like that."

He returned to his bed. Did she really, really care for him?

Chapter Eight

"You don't want to bother your mother with things like that, Princess. Just let her be. We're all right as things are. The new treatment's been just fine. She can always go back again if it's not," said Reg Perkins.

Rosie looked at her father. Her mother must have spoken to him about what she had said. "It's no big deal," she mumbled.

"What's that?" He spoke roughly. Rosie made no reply. "You leave her be. Everything's all right. Things are fine as they are."

Why had her mother told him? Why had she said anything to him? "I don't think everything is all right, Daddy. I think she's sick and I don't think it makes any difference when she goes to the hospital then comes home just to start all over again. I don't think I can do anything about it —

I don't think she would ever let me do anything about it. All I want is to know about it."

"We're all right as we are. Just leave things as they are," he repeated. "You don't understand." His voice hardened again.

"Why don't you want me to talk to her?" Rosie asked quietly. "Really, truly, why?"

Her father was getting angry. "It's none of your business. Understand?" They were the sharpest words she could remember from him. "You'll only make her sicker," he said. "I don't want her any worse than she is now."

In a strange way his anger pleased her and she made up her mind not to back off. Did it mean he really did care about her mother? Was there no way she could discover what he wanted for his wife? Find out what her mother wanted for herself? "I just want to know, that's all. She's my mother, and I want to know and I want to do something about it if there's anything I can do."

His temper evaporated and he spoke softly to her. "Princess, my little Princess, now don't you be bothering your pretty little head over such things as don't really matter. You do enough as it is. Daddy couldn't manage without Daddy's girl and that's all there is to it. You've got enough on your plate without putting your head in a whirl about your mother. What about your possum, then? How's he getting on, eh? Happy as a sandboy in that cage you've got him in. Talked away to me no end last time I took a look." He moved around the table toward her.

Rosie stiffened. She knew to expect the bear

hug and the caresses. Pretty little head, be damned. This was one day he wasn't going to pat or stroke it. Quickly she moved beyond his grasp and left the room.

"So, what d'you think of that then?" she asked Plum. "The old goat was telling me not to talk to her and to leave her alone. What do you think of that? I'm her daughter, for God's sake — she's my mother!" Delicately, almost monkeylike, the possum took a slice of banana from her and ate it. "I will talk to my own mother if I want to, Plum. How the hell can my talking to her make her any worse? There are things I've got to try and find out — things I'm going to find out. Why does she let him treat her the way he does?" The possum climbed her arm. Her claws were sharp and Rosie winced as they took hold. "You're getting bigger, Plum, much bigger. You're getting fatter, too." She stroked her pet. "I wonder what you think you are. Do you know you're a possum? I doubt it. What am I going to do with you, eh? I can't believe that you want to stay on here all your life, my little Princess." She spoke bitterly.

Quite happily, the possum left Rosie's arms and allowed itself to be deposited back in its cage.

As autumn progressed, Edith Perkins attacked her roses with more vigor than she had done for years. She stripped away the tangled undergrowth, cutting back the wilderness that bordered the lawns, and pruned the old rambling and climbing bushes to a more orderly state. At times, the energy of the woman was ferocious in its intensity and even though she wore gloves, her hands and arms became a network of criss-crossed scratches. She didn't seem to notice. Without pausing to eat, she would plunge into her garden as soon as she arrived home from the shop and would stay there until the darkness forced her inside. Her skin tanned in the autumn sun.

Rosie cooked and did as much of the housework as seemed necessary. She didn't mind; it was good to see her mother doing something in the afternoons other than sleep. From time to time, she thought uneasily that this behavior of her mother's was no more normal than that which had gone before.

"I think that is the last rose of summer, Rosa," said her mother, pointing out a lone, red bloom.

"There's a yellow one, too," Rosie said. "Just over there."

"It was a song, you know."

"What was?"

" 'The Last Rose of Summer.' It's still sung — you hear it on the wireless at times. Lovely song. Lovely flower."

"Did you really plant all these roses, Mother?" Rosie knew the answer but hoped to get her mother talking.

Edith smiled at her daughter. "I did indeed. All of them — when we first came here, your father and I.

Gather ye rosebuds while ye may,
Old Time is still a flying:
And this same flower that smiles today
Tomorrow will be dying.

Herrick. Elizabethan, you know. The rose is the most beautiful of the flowers. *La rose est des fleurs la plus belle.* French."

"I know," said Rosie.

"Of all of them only dear, old, lovely Dorothy Perkins was here when we came. Seemed to me an omen." Mrs. Perkins laughed. "How silly. Gather ye rosebuds, eh?"

"May I help you, Mother?"

Edith was startled. "Help me, Rosa? How could you possibly help me? Why? There's nothing to do. I've done it. It's all done now."

"With the roses, Mother. Can I help you with the roses?"

"I know what you mean, my dear," she said in a strained voice. "Come, we'll sit down. No. No, first you shall make us a nice pot of tea. Where is your father?"

"At work, Mother."

"Yes, of course. Then you make the pot of tea and I'll tidy away the last of this mess. Off you go now."

Rosie made the tea and prepared a tray with a cloth, biscuits and the good china. She carried it out to the lawn.

"Yes, lovely," said her mother with delight. "We'll play at being ladies in the rose garden."

They sat down and Rosie poured the tea. Edith began to talk. Part of what she said made absolutely no sense to Rosie. As a whole, it was a patchwork of bits and pieces; some to fit now, others later.

"I named you for the rose. There was no person

94

I wanted to name you after. I married your father and planted the roses. I have new tablets now, did you know that? They said they would trial them on me. Trial? They're for sleeping. I always liked this garden, that's why we bought this property. So very quiet. It didn't matter that we were hidden away down here and that we knew not a soul but each other. Didn't matter. We were, we are, solitary. You would understand that. You are, I know, very much the same. Oh, yes — I called you for the rose; of all flowers, the most beautiful."

She drank her tea, gazing out over the expanse of shadow-dappled lawn to the roses beyond. "It was a surprise to both of us when we discovered you were to be born. We were not young and a child was not something we had considered — not a part of us. I think . . ." She fell silent for a time as if knitting her thoughts, then spoke again. "Maybe it was that I tried to go on as if you had not come, were not there. Oh, you were fed and cared for — looked after. Of course you were." She was quiet again, reflecting.

"And then?" Rosie prompted very, very quietly.

"If they manage to make me sleep, they'll make it a smaller dose. Your father has the tablets and he gives them out to me." Edith nibbled around a biscuit. "You were such a silent baby. It was so easy to pretend you were not there. It still is." She shivered and pulled her old cardigan more closely about her thin shoulders as a cloud shrouded the sun. "There should have been nothing more. But then I was pregnant again. It wasn't easy. Not the same. It seemed years of waiting this time. Then he was born; your brother — my son. He lived for three months and he died. Dead. Just like that. As simple as that. Not like you — he wasn't like you. For three months he raged and hollered and cried and was angry. Just so alive. And, as if in return for all the trouble he had been in the making, he was beautiful. And he died. He died and it was as if I had no children."

"You still had me," said Rosie. "What about me?"

"There would be no others. I was far, far too old. Too old even for the two I had. The doctor said . . . it doesn't matter, I forget what he said. Your father cared for you. His girl, his little Princess. I was sick. So sick. Headaches — migraines. God, the headaches. All I could do was hold my head and rock for hours. So I drank. Not much; just a little at first. Then more."

They sat, and the shadows stretched further across the garden. "You had treatment?" Rosie asked.

"Oh, yes, I had treatment. Until the headaches had gone or were dulled into something . . . I don't know, dulled into something more deadly? I don't know. The drink helped."

"Where do you go, Mother? Where do you go when you go away?"

"I thought you knew. Has your father not told you?"

"No, I don't know. You tell me."

"I go to a psychiatric hospital — a mental hos-

96

pital, Rosa. I have treatment there, and it works for a short while. They give me therapy of one sort or another and treat my drinking. Alcoholism is what it is. I'm a drunk. A rose by any other name . . . ?" She began to sound impatient. "Why do you want to know all this, anyway? What difference does it make? What does it matter what they do? They say they need me for longer but I have to get away, leave the place. I get tired of it. I'm all right now, though, see? I'm quite all right." She stood up.

Rosie looked at the thin figure of her mother. The straight, grey hair and the pinched face. She saw an older image of herself, really, except for the eyes. Those of the woman were a wasted, slate grey, washed of most life.

"Leave it be, now. There's nothing else to tell you. Take these things in now and get on with whatever you have to get on with. Your father . . . I want to finish up here. I'm all right, really I am."

"Is there nothing I can do to help?" Rosie's voice was desolate. "I mean — is there nothing I can do to *really* help?"

"What do you mean, girl? Really help? You can do these dishes to really help. That's all. Come on, now, it's cold. I'll leave this till tomorrow — I want to lie down. Come on, quickly now."

"Do your parents drink?" Rosie asked Michael as they walked home.

"Yep. All the time. Just like fishes. Always on the juice, you've no idea. You must've heard them

97

from your place. When Dad's hitting the booze and Mum's hitting Dad . . . whew! I just go and hide under me bed."

Rosie could not believe him. "Come on, Michael, I was serious. You are joking, aren't you?"

"Me? Joke? Never." He sounded serious. "It's sheer hell. I've often thought I should tell the Welfare."

"You *are* joking. It's nothing to joke about," chided Rosie. She walked more quickly away from him up the road. It was too cold these days to sit on the verge. The leaves, not yet turned color, hung, a tired and tattered green.

"Okay, then, I was joking. Seeing as you're interested, Dad has a jug or two at the Club once a week with his mates after work. If my brothers are home, he takes them down, too — won't take me, but. No matter how hard I try. Mum? She only drinks a glass of wine sometimes. She signed a pledge at church when she was a girl but I think a priest told her a glass of wine is okay sometimes, but not to go overboard on the gin. Now me, well, that's a different — "

"Don't be stupid. You don't drink, and I don't think you smoke. Besides, didn't you once tell me something about wrecking the temple of your body?" She looked him up and down. "Though, if you ask me . . ."

"Why d'you want to know all this? About my old man and old lady?"

"Just interested, that's all," said Rosie.

"Oh, yeah?" He was unconvinced.

"How's your football coming on?"

"Rugby? Now, I know you're not interested in that!"

"Of course I am." Rosie gave him a smile.

"Liar! You're trying to get me off the other subject. My mum does that, too, when I ask her questions about sex," laughed Michael.

"I thought you knew it all," Rosie teased.

"Well, if that's the case, there sure isn't much to it then!" He laughed again.

"I happen to think it's important for friends to take an interest in what each other is doing, even if they have no personal interest in that thing themselves."

"Eh?"

"How is your precious football?"

"We've got a game next week. Come and see for yourself, seeing as how you're so interested."

"Me? Watch football? You must be joking!"

"Look, everyone else comes except you and about two others. We're the pride of the school, Old Jackson says. Besides, I'd like you to come. Really."

"All right," said Rosie, "I will."

"Good. Now, let's get back to things being important between two friends, like what you said — what's on your mind?"

"Nothing. Nothing at all, really," said Rosie, evasively.

"You're a liar, Perkins. I think I know what it is, anyway," said Michael.

"You don't! No, you don't," she snapped at him.

"Hey — it's all right. Just remember, if you do need to talk to someone, you can count on me. You know I wouldn't tell anyone. Have I ever let you down since we got to know each other? Have I?"

"No, of course you haven't," said Rosie. "But it hasn't been all that long since I got to know you."

"I think you could talk to my mum, too," he said. "She likes you."

"I don't need to talk to anyone, Michael, honest I don't. There's nothing. Nothing."

He was unconvinced.

Chapter Nine

Summer lingered on and on, in fits and starts, to a late Easter. The leaves on the big poplars that bordered half of Old Dump Road eventually changed color. Gold, yellow, orange; drifting in gusts and blusters as rising winds bared the branches. The leaves eddied ceaselessly on the little-used road, and frequently now the roadway was fully smothered in autumn. Rosie and Michael made the most of the lingering warmth.

She watched him play rugby and knew he was pleased. Pleased that she was there to see him and proud of his game.

"It's really the last place I thought I'd find you, Rosie," said Mrs. Geraghty, who had come to watch her son play. "I'm sure Michael told me you were not at all interested in sports."

"I'm not, Mrs. Geraghty. He asked me to come

101

and watch. I've very little idea of what they're doing!" Rosie was completely honest. "It's the first game of football I've ever seen."

"One is much the same as another," said Mrs. Geraghty. "I know that doesn't sound very loyal but it sure comes from the heart. I must've had about thirty years of it since I first watched Michael's father play, and then all his brothers. Can't really give up on the last one, now can I? Be just my luck when this one's done his dash to have to turn around and start supporting grandchildren. There were times, dear, when if I wasn't praying for rain, I was at least hoping one of them just might take up a different game. Do you really not know what they're doing, dear? You must have played some sport yourself?"

Rosie pulled a comical smile. "I know every trick there is for getting out of it. If it happens that I just can't — well, then I do some praying, too. I pray that the ball won't come in my direction!" She smiled again. "I think I do sort of roughly know what they're trying to do . . . common sense tells me the red ones want to go one way and the blue ones want to go the other!"

Mrs. Geraghty laughed. "There you go! That's all there is to it, really. You take my word. There's only one snag, though. They always, always take about an hour and a half trying to sort it out! Sometimes, in the middle of winter, that seems just about forever."

Almost against her will, Rosie found herself enjoying the match. Although her understanding was limited, she could see that Michael was quite good. Quick, alert, agile. Always there when the others appeared to need him.

"I hope you realize I gave up a good book for your football, Mick." Rosie stressed the nickname that she had not used before. "Get in there, Mick! Come on, Mick!" She laughed. "I hardly consider it worth the sacrifice," she kidded him.

"Oh, yeah? It was a great game and you really enjoyed it. Better'n any book, any day. Saw you standing with Mum. Pity the old man couldn't've been there. He played senior rugby for years."

"So your mother told me."

"Yeah, I saw you talking. Told you last week she really likes you."

"You sound surprised!" said Rosie.

A smile crossed Michael's face. "She reckons you're an improvement on Freddy and Cal any day!"

"Watch it! I'll kick you," she threatened.

"Whew! Gee, into sports already and you've only seen one game. You quiet ones are all the same — violent as anything underneath. Tough as guts, under it all."

"Being tough as guts, Michael, is quite, quite different from being violent."

"If you say so, Rosa. What else did you talk about with my old lady?"

"Oh, this and that . . . about her great love for sport — especially rugby."

"Yeah, I know — it's a bit of a worry. Last time they were home my brothers and Dad were saying

103

how when I finish with rugby, poor old Mum'll have nothing to watch."

In the hours just before dawn on Good Friday, Edith Perkins emptied the bottle of sleeping pills into half a glass of sherry. She swallowed the lot.

Rosie, unable to wake her mother for her early morning cup of tea, called her father from his room.

"She'll just be sleeping soundly," was all he said.

"No, she's not. The bottle of her tablets is here and there's nothing in it."

"She's just asleep, Princess."

Rosie threw off his hand as he touched her arm. "She's not asleep. Not asleep at all. Call the doctor."

He saw the look on her face. She stood right beside him as he made the phone call and explained the urgency.

Rosie watched as her mother was loaded into the ambulance. She watched as it left, its siren screaming, with her father in his truck right behind. She would not go with him and there were too many strangers around for him to try and make her.

She shivered in the cold, half light of the grey morning and pulled her robe closer around her. She found no warmth. She continued to stand, staring into the empty black tunnel of the driveway.

What had happened? What had her mother done? What had been done to her mother? Not knowing what she was doing, she walked slowly across the heavily-dewed grass in the direction taken by the ambulance. She no longer felt the cold. "I tried, Mummy. I did try," she said. And then she cried.

Returning to the house, Rosie went to her mother's room where she spent a long time straightening the bed, tidying away and ordering her mother's possessions. Then she sat and waited.

It was late morning when her father returned. "How is she?" asked Rosie.

"She's going to be all right, Princess."

"Where is she?"

"In the hospital. She'll be there — they'll keep her there for a few days . . ."

"And then she'll come home?"

"Well . . ."

"What do you mean? She will come home?" Rosie was insistent.

"Well, they'll probably send her back to the other hospital," her father explained. "They might keep her there for some time."

"The psychiatric hospital? The mental hospital?"

"How did you know that? I didn't know you knew," he said. "Yes, she'll be there for some time, I should think." He looked hard at her. "Don't you worry your pretty little head, Princess. We'll be all right."

"I'm not worried about *us* being all right," said Rosie. "It's my mother I'm worried about. How did she get those pills?"

"They gave them to her last time. They were a new sort," said Reg.

"I know what they are." Rosie's lips were tightly thin and her voice was cold. "Mother told me she had them. She also told me that she didn't keep them, that they were given to you to give her as she needed them."

"Come on, Princess. You're upset. You don't know anything about it," he said.

"Okay, so how did she get the sherry? All that sherry out there that she didn't need. I've seen it. It's all out there now — cartons of the bloody stuff! She never got that for herself, did she?"

"Stop it now, Princess, you're upsetting yourself. Now don't you be going on about things you know nothing about. We'll be all right, Princess, you'll see."

"I told you, Daddy, I don't care about us being all right. You and me, we are all right. I care about my mother being all right, that's what I care about." Rosie turned away from her father.

"Princess . . ." he began.

She turned on him angrily. "Don't you ever, ever, ever call me Princess again. Do you understand?" She left him.

Easter was the center of Norma Geraghty's year. Better even than Christmas with its heat, the worry about presents and whether or not she was going to have enough money to meet the expectations of her boys; expectations that grew as the boys grew. Easter was different. Easter was the true heart of her church-being, her mother-being.

106

It had been good when her boys were small, but it seemed even better now that they were grown and they all came home to be together. The older boys would arrive home on the Thursday night in time for them all to attend Mass together at the old wooden church in the center of Cooper's Junction. Her family took up an entire pew in the little church on this day, the first of several occasions of worship over the days of Easter. The season renewed her faith and strength and freshened her love for her family. That her men were not as enthusiastic as she about attending every Easter service at St. Joseph's, she could accept. Once or twice during the long weekend, she would leave them asleep at home and walk in the chill morning to attend the earliest Mass. At such times she enjoyed the quiet, the cold and the loneness.

It was at just such a time in the early morning of Good Friday that she was forced to the side of the road by the ambulance carrying Edith Perkins. She stood, puzzled, as the vehicle rushed by, its siren wailing as a warning to anything that may be out so early on the winding road. Then, moments later, her neighbor's truck also shot by.

Norma Geraghty arrived home worried and concerned.

"Could be anything," said her husband, still in bed.

"It could hardly be just anything, dear. If it wasn't coming from here, it had to be coming from there."

"Makes sense," he smiled at her.

"You know what I mean. Anyway, I'm worried. Don't say anything to the boys."

"I wasn't going to."

"Of course not. Still," she brightened, "you were going to get breakfast for them, weren't you? You did say."

"They're big enough and ugly enough to get breakfast for themselves," he grunted as he gathered the blankets more closely about him, pretending deep sleep.

"I am worried, dear. I'm going to make some enquiries," said his wife.

Realizing that he didn't have a chance of snoozing off and that the business of the ambulance really had concerned his wife, Stan Geraghty reluctantly got out of bed. "Leave it alone, Norm," he advised. "We don't even know them."

"You know I can't do that. What if it's Rosie? Think of Michael. Besides, it would be quite, quite wrong to leave it alone."

"I still say leave it alone," he repeated.

Norma Geraghty "left it alone" for a further half hour, then made two or three phone calls through the network of her nearest and dearest friends, giving serious thought to the information she needed before making each call. By the time she had finished her sons were up and about, woken to the call of bacon and eggs. She beckoned to her husband to follow her to their bedroom.

"It's Edith Perkins. She's overdosed. She's in the hospital now, but they're taking her off somewhere else on Monday. I phoned Betty Smith — she's still night Staff Nurse over there — and she

108

was just coming off duty when they brought the poor soul in. I'm going over to see if there's anything I can do."

"To the hospital?" said her husband.

"Don't be silly, of course not . . . to their place, the Perkins place."

"Keep out of it, Norm, love. They — well, he — Reg Perkins won't want our help."

Norma Geraghty looked at her husband incredulously. "It's not him I'm thinking of — it's the girl."

"You're biting off more than you can chew, girl. We tried once, years ago. They showed us then where we could shove our friendship."

"That was then. This is now and circumstances change. I can't do otherwise. I'll take the car. Not a word to Michael, all right?"

Her husband could not persuade her not to go. "I don't know what on earth you think you can do," he said as she left.

She did not really know either. As she pulled into her neighbor's driveway she wished for a moment that she'd taken her husband's advice.

Rosie answered the back door and her neighbor walked into the kitchen without waiting for an invitation. Rosie sat down at the kitchen table opposite her father. Norma guessed they had been sitting like this for some time. "I've just heard that Edith is ill and has been taken to the hospital. Is there anything I can do to help?" She stood, nervous. Reg Perkins did not invite her to sit.

"No thank you, we're all right. There's nothing you can do." He stood.

109

Nervous she may have been but a family of sons had taught her over the years never to take a first refusal. She looked at Rosie and thought that she may have been crying. Whether she had or not, Norma could see that Rosie was very tense, tight within herself.

"Then you'll be wanting to spend some time with her at the hospital, Reg, I'm sure. Perhaps Rosie would like to come home with me for a couple of days. Would you, Rosie?"

"She'll be all right as she is. No," Reg answered, "thank you for asking. We'll manage as we are." He stayed standing and nodded toward the door.

"I think that is very kind of you, Mrs. Geraghty," said Rosie quietly. "I will come, thank you. I'd like that."

"You're going nowhere, girl," Reg moved to the door.

Rosie fixed her father in her clear stare and said, "I'm going with Mrs. Geraghty, Daddy. She's right. You can spend as much time at the hospital as you like without having to bother about me. I'll come home on Sunday and come and see Mummy with you. You said she probably wouldn't be allowed to see me until then. I'll just get a couple of things to take with me to your place, Mrs. Geraghty." Rosie left the room.

"Please, if there is anything I can do to help, do let me know," Norma offered.

"You've done more than enough already." There was a bitter sound to his voice.

"She'll be fine," said Norma but did not make it clear whether she spoke of Rosie or her mother.

110

Perkins made no reply. Norma Geraghty shivered, and not from the cold of the room alone. Just like a museum, Mum, she remembered.

Rosie emptied everything from her schoolbag and packed those few things she imagined she would need for a two-day stay away from home. It wasn't until she was in the Geraghty car that she remembered. "Plum. I can't leave Plum."

"Plum?" Norma was anxious to get away and hoped the delay would not bring Rosie's father out.

"She's my possum — Michael knows her. I can't leave Plum behind." Rosie showed agitation for the first time.

"No, of course you can't, dear. You go and get it — we'll find somewhere for Plum." She wasn't entirely sure just where. "Do you need a hand?"

"No, no — she knows me. I won't be long." Rosie stuffed Plum into the bag with her other belongings and zipped it up so that only her head and neck showed. "She'll be all right in there," she said. "It's only for a little drive."

Norma hoped she was right. The idea of a possum tearing apart the interior of the car was not one that would go down well with her husband. However, the animal gave no indication that she found the drive anything out of the ordinary and calmly nestled her head into the crook of Rosie's arm.

Reg Perkins had stayed within the house.

Chapter Ten

Room was found for Rosie. Brendan was put in with Patrick and Sean was already sharing with Michael. Room was also found for Plum. Patrick remembered a cage he had built years before for guinea pigs, and dragged it out from under the house. Plum showed that she felt quite at home and allowed the whole family to stroke her and play with her before taking up temporary accommodation in the hastily repaired cage. "One good thing about having carpenters for sons, Rosie," said Mr. Geraghty, "is that they can make things."

"Which reminds me," his wife chipped in. "I've made a list of things for while they're at home. Odds and ends I need doing."

"Aw, Mum," moaned Patrick. "You and your lists. We're home for a holiday — anyway, I've brought my new shotgun home. Me and Brendan wanna go up to the old dump and try it out on a few bunnies."

"You'll do no such thing! It's Easter. You'll not shoot anything at Easter," said his mother.

"Not even the Easter Bunny?" joked Brendan. His mother shut him up with a look.

"I only wanted to try it out," said Patrick. "It's duck shooting season in a week or so."

"To the very best of my knowledge, rabbits don't fly. Besides, I've said no," their mother said firmly.

The boys knew there was no room for further argument. "Okay, give us your list," sighed Brendan. "Seems to me it'll only take another couple of years and Patrick and I will have built you a completely new house!"

"I'm glad you see things my way, and that's a nice thought, dear. Now, I must get on with lunch. Sean!" she called. "You get in here — it's time you gave me a hand. Michael! You take Rosie out for a while and have a look around."

Michael had said little. His pleasure at seeing Rosie was mixed with the sudden surprise of her arrival. He could only guess that all was not right. Rosie's silences, her stillness at times — neither were new to him, however he felt there was more to it this time.

"You want to tell me about it?" he asked as they wandered away from the house.

"There's not much to tell," she replied.

"There must be something," he said. "You're here. I didn't count on seeing you till next week and now here you are! And I reckon it's not just because you wanted to come and stay."

113

"My mother's in the hospital."

"Why? What'd she do?" asked Michael.

"What d'ya mean, what did she do? She's sick and she's in the hospital, that's all." She paused. "God, what the hell. Yes, it is what she did. She took all her pills — her new ones. I don't know what they were or anything about them. But she took them — the whole lot."

"Jeez! Tried to do herself in?"

"Kill herself? Yes, I think that's what she tried to do. Didn't work though." Rosie stood up from the log on which they sat. "My mother tried to kill herself — she didn't want to go on living. She wanted to stop living and I can't understand that."

"Who found her?"

"I did."

"Jeez . . . and your old man? What about him?"

Rosie looked down at him. "My old man should've been looking after the pills. Yet she got them and she took them. My old man saw that there was plenty of booze for her to wash them down . . ." She stopped.

"What're you trying to say?" Michael was puzzled.

"I don't know what I'm trying to say, Michael. I don't even know what I think. Was Daddy careless? Is that what I'm trying to say? Or am I saying that he doesn't give a damn? Do I think that it's easier for him to keep things the way they are rather than do anything about it? I just wish I knew. But I don't think I'll ever, ever know."

Michael did not know what to say. He did not know how to respond to what Rosie was saying

114

to him. "You've had it tough, eh?" was all he could come up with. And that didn't sound enough.

"Have I?" She looked at him. "I don't think I have — not really. My mother has had it tough. Maybe my father has had it tough, too. Do you know what?"

"No," he said.

"I want to cry," said Rosie.

"Go ahead — cry if you want to," he said awkwardly. He wanted to hold her, to comfort her, but didn't know how to go about it.

"But I can't cry," said Rosie. "I want to but I can't."

The noise of the family, the constant moving about, the blaring of stereo and radio, were all too much for Rosie to handle. She sat, silent, taking in the play around her.

She thought of her mother. She thought of her father — and wondered if he had gone to sit with his wife, if he had gone to see if she was all right. She did not think to call her father and there was no call from him.

"Would you like me to call the hospital for you?" Michael's mother asked her.

"It doesn't matter, really, Mrs. Geraghty." Rosie did not know what to say or what to do.

"I will anyway."

Edith Perkins was "satisfactory," as hospitals say. Rosie relaxed a little. The Geraghtys left her in Michael's care during the afternoon while they went to church to recite the Good Friday Stations of the Cross.

115

"Church is a big thing for your family, isn't it?" Rosie remarked to Michael.

"I suppose it is. Dad says us Micks never do anything by halves. Never think too much about it, really. Just do it. It's sort of a part of life."

"Do you think that's what keeps you all together as a family?" Briefly, Rosie wondered if it might be churchgoing, or rather the lack of it, that made her own family like it was.

"Aw, you know me," said Michael, "until you became part of my life I never really thought of things in that way. You know — questioning things. Seems you're forever on about how things work and why and all that. You never seem to take things just as they are. Us? We're a family, that's all. Just accept it. We're Catholics and we go to church. I don't know if that's what keeps us together or not. Probably there's some damn bad Micks who make bad families. See, I dunno. I really dunno, Rosa."

"Whew, as you would say, that's some long speech. Still, I know what you mean. It's just that so much here is so different from what I'm used to, that's all." She smiled at him.

"Sure is nice to see you smile, Rosa Dorothy Perkins."

"Not much to smile about today, Michael Joseph."

"Look . . . I dunno how to say this, Rosie . . . see, I do care about you. A helluva lot. One thing you've done for me is you've got me thinking. I don't know why I was such a bastard for so long — guess I'll never really know that. But now I can do your sort of thinking. I can think about you. Your family. What's happened to your mother is real sad. It is for you, too. I don't know how I can do anything to help you or to make it better, but I want to . . . I don't really know how to say all this," he paused slightly, "to say all this properly." He looked down at his feet.

"I think you say it quite well, Michael. I do."

Gently, unsure of himself, Michael moved his arm around her back and they sat, quietly, side by side. She felt his arm about her and liked the feel of it. They sat together in silence for a long time.

The others returned and the day drew in. Everyone worked together helping to get the dinner. The noise was no less — if anything, it grew — but, for Rosie, in some way it became easier to bear. Just being there, a part of them, a part of what Michael's family was. Jokes; loud, long and always laughed at. The sounds of eating; and it seemed to Rosie that they never quite stopped. Continual horsing around; the boys teasing, pushing and punching each other, all in fun. Above and beyond it all, the parents, fully used to it, just quietly going about the lion's share of whatever work was to be done.

There was a brief lull as the quietest, Sean, said grace before their meal. This was a sign, as far as Rosie could see, less of thanks than as a sign for things to get even louder.

"What'll your possum eat, Rosie?" Stan Geraghty asked her. "Better be finding him something before this lot eat their mother and me out of house and home."

"It's a her, actually, Mr. Geraghty," said Rosie. "She seems to eat anything these days. Michael tells me it's so's she can put on condition for the winter."

"It's a fine pet, Rosie," said Sean. "I had a chat to her before dinner. Where'd you find her?"

"On the road — just on the side of the road. Her mother had been run over."

"You're very clever to have reared it," he said.

Rosie smiled at him. "Not really. I did try hard but I think it was more good luck than anything in particular I did."

"Your possum must have wanted very much to live," said Sean.

"I suppose so," she replied.

"It's not all that hard," Michael objected.

"How would you know?" retorted Sean. "You spend most of your waking hours killing the poor things, not rearing them."

"That's unfair, Sean," his father scolded. "You should know better."

There was an uncustomary hush, then Rosie turned back to Sean and said, "Do you mind if I ask you a question?"

"Of course not," said Sean, feeling slightly dented by his father's words. Everybody else remained quiet at the prospect of Rosie's question.

"Once — a long time ago — did you shoot our chickens?"

All eyes turned to Sean. He blushed dramatically in a way only redheads can. The color rose

118

fully up his face. He looked at his plate then up to the ceiling as if looking for guidance.

Mrs. Geraghty's mouth opened and she gulped. "I don't think . . . Rosie, I'm sure Sean . . . not Sean." Surely not Sean.

"Whew!" he said. And Rosie knew now from whom his younger brother got the expression. "Whew! Well, um . . . yes, I did."

"Sean! Sean, I never knew," said his mother.

"It wasn't exactly the sort of thing I could come home and tell you, Mum. Well, not then. It was a long time ago, Mum — years and years ago."

"See, I knew I was right," said Rosie to Michael, "and you said it couldn't be him."

They all laughed, Mrs. Geraghty not quite as cheerfully as the others. They poked and play punched at Sean.

"Only thing he could ever hit would have to be in a pen!"

"Awful shot he was — could never hit anything."

"Oh, they weren't in pens," said Rosie. "They ran everywhere. I remember. It was, I think, a very good shot. But I knew it was you, Sean. I saw you."

Michael and Rosie cleared the table while the others leaned back, overfull, in their chairs. Rosie thought it was just about the most enjoyable meal she had ever had. It didn't even take her long to get used to the level of noise.

Later, she lay wide awake in bed and thought of her mother. No happy Easter for her — no Easter at all, in fact. "There must be some way,

Mummy, for you to let me do something to help you through all this." She sat up in bed, drew her knees up to her chin and spoke softly to herself. "You can come through this, I just know you can. And I know I can help — if you'll only let me. You can't, can't, can't want to die. Please let me help you . . ."

Much later, Norma Geraghty checked on Rosie. The girl was asleep. Gently the woman straightened and tucked in the bedding that Rosie, restless, had tossed from her. She bent down, smoothed Rosie's hair against her pillow and kissed her lightly. Rosie stirred slightly but did not waken. "Poor little soul," the woman murmured. "Sleep well and God bless." She quietly left the room.

Chapter Eleven

On Easter Sunday Rosie walked home, alone except for the possum tucked away, pouchlike, in the front of her jacket. She could tell from the rush and bustle of breakfast that morning, the hasty ironing of best clothes and the talk, that this day would be the highlight of the Geraghtys' weekend — Easter Day. Norma Geraghty had offered to take her home. Michael said he would walk with her. Patrick and Brendan each offered to drive her in their very old cars. She insisted on going alone.

"Thank you for a lovely time, Mrs. Geraghty." They were alone in the little bedroom as Rosie packed her belongings.

"Listen to me, Rosie," said Norma Geraghty, facing the girl and holding her lightly at the elbows. "Now listen. If ever you need me for any-

thing, at any time, don't you hesitate for one minute to call me. Now I mean that. For any reason
at all, d'you hear? You are more than welcome
to come and stay with us any time you want." She
hesitated for a moment. "Or any time you need
to, understand? I'll pop in and see your father
when his shop opens after the break and I'll be
telling him the same." She smiled. "And don't you
think, now, that I'd be doing it just for your sake —
I'd love to have you stay, really I would. I'm not
just saying that. It gets a bit lonely for one woman
in a houseful of men. So you see you'd actually
be doing me a big favor." She laughed. "I could
even give you some more lessons on the finer
points of the game of rugby!"

"Thank you, Mrs. Geraghty. I will remember."

"You'd better, Rosie, otherwise I'll be coming
to get you. I always mean what I say. Now I must
away — if I don't go now, God knows what Brendan will be wearing for church!"

Michael walked Rosie to the gate. "You be okay
now?" he asked.

"I'm all right. Thanks for everything, Michael."

"Think nothing of it. I'll be sending the account
next week," he joked.

"You would, too! No — no you wouldn't." She
smiled. "And I do love your family, they're wonderful."

"Guess they're okay," was all he said. He thought
of saying something along the lines of not mind-
ing if she *liked* them, but would rather she saved
her love for him. He was too shy.

Rosie just smiled. "See you, then." She tucked Plum more securely into her jacket and wandered off down the road. Michael watched until she was out of sight.

"Okay, Plum, let's you and me get back to our home," she said softly, grimly to her pet.

Her father was at home in the kitchen, almost as if he had not moved since she left. "Your mother's all right," he said before she could ask. He mentioned nothing about her weekend.

"I know. Mrs. Geraghty phoned the hospital and they told her," said Rosie. She looked at him. "You have been to see her?"

"Yes," he said, "yes, I have."

"Have you had any breakfast?" she asked.

"No. Not yet."

"Then I'll make us some. When can we go and visit Mummy?"

"It's little use going. She just lies there. She doesn't say anything."

"I want to go," said Rosie.

"We'll go this afternoon," he replied.

Rosie prepared their food quickly and neatly while her father sat and watched her. He said nothing. They ate in silence and Rosie thought to herself of the difference between her home and the Geraghty home. She had lived here, in this house, all her life. And now, today, it seemed less like a home than ever.

"Nothing is ever as you think it might be, Rosie," said her father.

"What do you mean?"

123

"You wouldn't understand," he said.

"You could try to help me understand, Daddy," she said. But he would say no more.

"I don't want to go in. If you want to see her, you go." Her father's words were unexpected. They sat in the cab of the truck in the parking area at the hospital.

She said nothing for a moment, then, "You have been to see her though? You have visited Mummy, haven't you?"

"Yes," he said dully, "she's all right."

Rosie got out of the vehicle, slammed the door, then leaned back through the window to speak to him. "Where is she?"

"Ward One. Room to herself — you'll see it."

It was a small, country hospital. Only thirty beds. Finding her mother was not difficult. Edith Perkins was sitting up in bed. She had a magazine in her lap but was not reading. Instead, she stared out over the frost-browned flower beds to the rolling, hazy hills of the horizon. Into the distance.

"Hello, Mother."

"Rosa?" Her mother wrinkled her forehead. "What are you doing here? Shouldn't you be at school?"

"It's Sunday, Mother. Anyway, it's Easter."

"Easter? Of course it is — how silly of me. I seem to have lost all track . . ."

"How are you, Mother?"

"Quite all right, thank you, Rosa."

They sat. Rosie could not think of anything to say. The woman in the bed had nothing to say.

124

Two, three minutes. A long time. Edith Perkins' fingers plucked at a fold in the bedspread. Her eyes focused — or unfocused — on what lay beyond the window. Her mother looked just the same, Rosie thought. Distant and withdrawn. Unreachable. Her whole thin, gray being was like a vacant shell.

The room was bright with a thin sunlight striking the pale surfaces. The only color was from a vase of roses. A small card was propped against the vase and Rosie read, *Get well soon. Kind thoughts, the Geraghty family.* She wondered if her mother had seen the flowers or read the card. She wondered when Mrs. Geraghty had found time to think of a gift.

"D'you want a cup of tea, dear?" said a nurse entering the room. She did not wait for a reply. "Yes, of course you do. No milk and two sugars if I remember rightly, and my word, that mower of ours is going just fine since your Reg looked at it for us. And what about you, dear?" To Rosie. "Would you like one, too? Good. Now, how would you like it? Biscuits today, dear." To Edith. "Easter, you know. The staff's little treat for you all. Don't usually have biscuits anymore — not these days. Cutting back left, right and center. Here we are, then. Comfy?" And she was off with a clatter.

"Is there anything I can do, Mother?" Rosie asked.

Her mother dragged her eyes away from the distant view, and with a conscious effort addressed herself to the girl at her bedside. "I don't think so, Rosa. I'm all right. Really, I am all right. A

125

pity it all happened the way it did . . . Tomorrow, or some day, they'll send me back . . . back? I don't know." She looked at her vase of flowers. "I don't know where those came from. Not my garden, I think. Hot house blooms, surely." She spoke in brief and hurried spurts of words, pausing between each phrase as if her little statements were complete thoughts.

"Mr. and Mrs. Geraghty sent them."

"Did they? Goodness!"

"I stayed with them after you came here," said Rosie.

"Did you really? You stayed with them? What on earth was your father thinking of? I don't know. I'm tired."

Please let me help you, Mother. Please let me get through to wherever you are. Please let me touch you in some way. Rosie didn't speak her thoughts. She sat, head bowed, her fingers also playing with the bed cover, folding and pleating. Then her mother took her hand in a completely unexpected gesture. She held it tightly and the girl squeezed in return. "Old time is still a-flying, eh?" Mrs. Perkins gave a small laugh.

"I think so, Mummy," said Rosie, smiling at her mother. "Get better, Mummy. Please get better."

Her mother said nothing more. Rosie left soon after.

April dragged cold into May and the first snows rimmed the distant mountains. Life was little changed for Rosie. Routines stayed the same. Her father seldom mentioned her mother. "She'll be

126

away for some time," was all he said.

"Can we go and see her?" Rosie sometimes asked.

"We'll see," he would say.

School seemed to press in on her and she looked forward to the May holidays in a way she had not done before. An escape? Two days before the term ended, Rosie was sitting in the library reading. A girl came and sat down beside her.

"Mum and Dad have said I can have a party in the holidays. Me and some of the others thought you might like to come." She spoke in a rush. Rosie said nothing. "If you're not going away or anything, that is," said the other. "Dad's going to clean out the garage and we can make as much noise as we like. What d'you say?"

"Thank you."

"Micky's coming. Well, I sure hope he is. You, too."

"Is he?" said Rosie. Michael had not mentioned it to her.

"As I said, it's in the garage. No dressing up — just jeans and things."

"Thank you," repeated Rosie. "I'll ask my father and then I'll let you know."

The girl looked puzzled. Ask her father? "Yeah. Well, we'd like for you to come." She left.

A day later Mrs. Geraghty called in. Rosie was home alone, her father was not yet in from the shop. "You've not been to see us, Rosie. Now, I did say."

Saying was all well and good, Rosie thought — how do you just drop in? "Yes, Mrs. Geraghty, I'm sorry."

"No need to be sorry, my dear." She looked at Rosie and guessed at her difficulties. "You just come. Turn up whenever you like — you'll always be welcome. Now then, here's some baking; a few biscuits and a cake to put in your tins. Made far too much for just the three of us." She piled her load on the table. "Now, what are you doing about the holidays?"

"What am I doing about the holidays?" Rosie asked.

"Yes, dear," Norma laughed, "that's what I said. We'd love to have you come and stay. There'll just be Dad and Michael and me, of course."

"I don't think — " began Rosie.

"Would you like me to speak to your father?" Norma asked.

"No. No, I don't think so."

"I won't take no for an answer," said the woman, smiling.

"I think it would be better if I didn't, Mrs. Geraghty. Honestly, I think it would only cause trouble. Would it be all right instead if I just came over some days to see you?" she asked. "When Daddy's away at work?"

"Of course, child. Whatever you like. We'd far rather have you staying, but if you think it's better . . . Well, if you don't pop over, I'll be coming to get you, make no mistake about it!"

"I'll come," Rosie smiled.

"How is your mother?"

"I think she's all right," replied Rosie.

"You've not been to see her lately?"

"There hasn't been much time."

128

Norma Geraghty looked at Rosie. "I'll tell you what — if you ever want to go and see her and — er — your father — well, if you can't, you just let me know. I'll take you, I'd be only too happy."

Norma looked around the dark, drab kitchen. "Is there anything else you need, my dear?" A touch of desperation in her voice.

"I don't think so."

"Well, before I go, you can show me that lovely little possum of yours again? Peach? Have I got it right? Dear wee thing."

"It's Plum, Mrs. Geraghty. Not that I think she would know the difference. She even answers to the name Michael sometimes."

"All I can say to that is it's more than the gentleman himself often does!" She chuckled. "Come on then, let's go and see your Plum. You're quite sure there's nothing else you need?"

"No. No, there isn't," said Rosie.

"Well, my little love, I think there is one thing you jolly well need." And without saying more, she took the girl in her arms and gave her a good, big hug. "There now. And I must say you're a darn sight smaller than any of my tribe. Come on, now. Let's find this possum."

By hook or by crook, Norma Geraghty thought to herself, she'd get Rosie to her home for at least a couple of days during the holidays.

Chapter Twelve

"There's no way I can go, Michael. No way would he ever let me go and I'm not even going to ask him. That's all there is to it."

"You've gotta ask him. How can you know he won't let you go if you don't even ask? Go on, Rosie, at least ask. I want you to go," pleaded Michael.

"It's no use, Michael. Besides — I know it sounds silly, but I've got nothing to wear."

"No one's going fancy," he said. "It's only a couple of hours in someone's garage. I know he won't say no."

"Anyway, I'm not stupid enough to think they really want me there," said Rosie.

"Of course they want you there. That's why you got asked. If you don't go, I won't go."

"That's why I got asked," said Rosie. She smiled

at him. "Everything is so easy for you. You don't understand. Your life is all so normal and easy — too easy for you to ever understand that it can be different for other people. Even now that I like you so much, there are still little moments when I actually hate you for how easy you've got it. It's almost as if the whole world is designed for people like you to make it to wherever you want to go without any sort of struggle at all."

"I'm sorry," Michael apologized, not really knowing what he'd done wrong.

"Oh, all right, I'll try. God knows he'll never agree. Do you know, this week, he hasn't even spoken to me more than one or two words. Eats his meals — whatever I feed him — then off he goes. You could never understand that. Never, never. Anyway, I'll try."

"Why do you want to go?" her father asked.

"They invited me to go. It's only for one or two hours. Pauline phoned again today and said not to worry about getting home, her mother and father always drop everyone off."

"Do you want to go?"

"Yes. I would like to go," said Rosie.

"Go then. Go if you want. Can't for the life of me think why you want to — damn fool rubbish." He smiled at her. "Seems to me, if you want to be gadding out with all your girlfriends, you'd better step out in style, Princess." Rosie gritted her teeth. So — there'd be a price to pay. Well, she'd pay it. She said nothing. "You come into the shop tomorrow and I'll give you some money.

131

Find yourself a party frock. Something real nice. It'll be good to see you all dolled up."

The next morning she walked the hill track to the Geraghtys'. "You said to call — here I am," she said to Mrs. Geraghty.

"And not before time, either," the woman replied with obvious delight. "You come right on in. Michael!" she called. "Rosie's here!"

"I'm allowed to go to the party!" Rosie said in a rush. "And I'm allowed to buy something to wear." She giggled excitedly. "I can't believe it. He said I could go and I can't believe it!"

"I told you so," said Michael coming into the room.

"Now, then," said his mother, "what on earth are we going to get for you to wear?"

"Oh, it's just jeans," said Rosie. "I'll buy a pair and I've got a jersey for on top."

"I think you may have a lot to learn, Rosie," said Mrs. Geraghty. "In my experience it never is 'just jeans.' Would you like me to come with you to find something?" Looking Rosie up and down, she could see that a helping hand would be in order. The girl may well have a large measure of strange and unusual beauty, but she had no measure at all of dress sense. "How about we have a bite of lunch here, then go off to the shops?" She did not wait for a reply.

"Can I come, too?" asked Michael.

"No," said his mother, "you can stay and do the dishes. Besides, Rosie and me want this as a surprise, don't we, Rosie?"

132

"Yes . . . no . . . I don't know," said Rosie. She didn't know what to say.

"Now," said Norma Geraghty to herself. "Who shall I ring? I've simply got to find out what's being worn to this thing. Why didn't God give me a daughter? Claudia's mother should know. Really, this is so exciting!"

"Huh! It's not making me feel too great," complained Michael. "Like, first I get to do all the dishes, then get blamed for not being a girl."

"Yes," said his mother absentmindedly. "Now you set the table while I rustle up something to eat."

Norma Geraghty decided to tackle Reg Perkins. "Rosie tells me she's on her way to buy one or two things." No need to let on just where Rosie had told her this news. "Just thought I'd be a real stickybeak and offer the child a hand — she didn't seem too clear about what she was after. You don't mind do you, Reg? I know this dear little place just down from the Post Office in the new mall. Be more than happy to pop the account round to you if that's all right with you?"

"If that's what Rosie wants . . ." There was a reluctance and uncertainty in his acceptance of her offer.

"Thank you, Daddy. Mrs. Geraghty is being very kind," said Rosie.

May as well kill two birds with one stone, thought Norma. "Now, I've already said to Rosie that if she's getting too lonely in that big house of yours while her mother's away, we'd be delighted to see more of her. We loved having her for those couple of days at Easter. No trouble at all."

"We're all right," said Reg Perkins.

"She's more than welcome," Norma prattled on, "and company for me, too."

The prices of clothes in the "dear little place" shocked Rosie. Was it really possible to spend this much on clothing? Mad! Quite mad. The woman in the shop seemed to be a good friend of Norma Geraghty and the two entered into a whispered debate. Rosie knew she was the subject under inspection.

There was nothing unusual about anything they bought. The jeans, well cut, were an excellent fit. "My word, you're a perfect stock size. Lucky thing, you!" The top was a loose-fitting, white sweat shirt in the latest style. A pair of flat, white, casual shoes completed the picture. Although each item alone was nothing special, the effect in total was something else again. Rosie could not believe her reflection in the long fitting room mirror. Norma looked over her shoulder. "Lovely," was all she said.

"Yes, it is," said Rosie with absolute honesty.

"Now we'll go see my hairdresser — a way with hair you'd never believe."

Rosie lifted a hand to her hair. "I . . . no — " she began.

"Don't you worry. Not a cut — just a tiny trim. Beautiful as it is, it'll fall even better. Then I'll just pop back and see your dad. I think it might be best for everyone if you stay overnight with us after the party. I'll just let your father know I can take you. Save him any trouble. Now . . . I know you haven't told him a lie — and I haven't either — but, my dear, he has absolutely no idea that boys will be there, has he? I'm also quite sure that he doesn't know you met me through your friendship with Michael — or, for that matter, that Michael exists at all. Am I right?"

Rosie blushed and nodded miserably. "Yes." The day seemed suddenly dulled.

She took Plum with her to the Geraghtys', secure in the knowledge that no one would mind and that the guinea pig cage would still be available. The animal's coat had thickened. While she was affectionate as ever with Rosie, there was now a restlessness about the young animal that had not shown before.

"You're going in this box whether you like it or not," said Rosie. "The way you've been behaving lately I wouldn't trust you for a minute in the front of my jacket this time. And stop squawking! You'll be perfectly happy once we get there, you were last time. Ouch!" The animal scratched her. "Stop it, damn you. I'm looking forward to this, even if you're not. Though you may well ask what on earth it is I'm looking forward to. Come on, now."

That Plum was now aware of her own kind was evident to Rosie. The old shed showed increasing signs of night visitations by other possums. Scratch marks were clear around the window, and there were often possum droppings on the ground. Plum was now a good three-quarters grown. Her fur

135

was lustrous and full as she faced none of the wear and tear experienced by her sisters of the wild. Frequently now, Rosie wondered what would become of her. Should she still be kept caged alone? Or would she eventually pine without the company of others of her kind? Would the needs that must be within her grow, fluctuate and wither? Rosie did not know the answers.

"Just the same as a bitch in heat," explained Michael, "or an unspayed cat with all the old toms hanging round. Have her fixed — same as you do with cats. Must be okay to be done."

"I've never heard of it. Besides, it doesn't seem very fair," said Rosie. "It's her nature."

"What's fair? It's not really fair keeping it caged up when it wants to get out and get at it."

"I'm positive she couldn't survive in the wild. You must know that. Nothing I could do would prepare her for that."

"Could be like that lion in Africa. There was this film on telly — "

"Elsa? Yeah, I know. Maybe it's easier with lions than with possums."

"I know which I'd rather deal with," said Michael. "You could start by taking her to a tree and yelling at her to climb. Go on, give it a go!"

"Full of bright ideas, aren't you? Still, your idea about having her fixed can't be as silly as all that." She looked at him, thinking.

"Yeah — can just see the look on the vet's face!" he hooted.

* * *

136

Michael was unprepared for the sight of Rosie on the night of the party. All he could say was, "Whew! You sure look good!"

Her classmates shared his surprise. There were looks, whispers and then greetings that she had never expected to hear from any of them. Even a few friendly smiles. The garage was a riot of color — streamers, balloons, posters, clothing. And sound. Michael stayed close to her, sensing just how new and strange everything must seem.

"Is it always like this?" she asked him.

"Like what?"

"The noise and all."

"Yeah — good, eh? She's got her brother's sounds and all his latest tapes. Great, eh? Whaddya reckon?"

"Great," said Rosie unsurely. "It's certainly loud. Does it ever stop?"

"What for?" He was surprised. The noise, to him, was no more than that needed for daily living. "Dance?" he offered.

"No!" she squeaked. "Dance? I couldn't do what they're doing. No way!" Noticing that most of the party seemed to be taking brief trips out of the garage, in twos and threes, she asked Michael, "What do they all keep going outside for? Is there something else out there?"

"You could say that. Reckon one or two of the guys have got a couple of bottles planted. Beer." He grinned. "They just hop out for a quick guzzle and probably a smoke. D'you want to take a look?"

"You haven't been out."

137

"Not yet."

"Why don't they bring it in here?" Rosie was puzzled.

"Oh, yeah, sure — and that'd be the end of it. Her old man and old lady are pretty strict, you know."

"Where are they, anyway? Why aren't they here?"

Michael sighed. "You really have to know it all, don't you? Look, I don't know. They're probably in the kitchen, sweating it out until we all go home, hoping like hell nothing goes wrong or that the cops don't come round coz the neighbors have complained about the noise."

"See — I knew it was noisy." Rosie sounded satisfied.

Cal and Fred came over to greet Michael and, for the first time ever, to talk socially with Rosie. "Good party, eh?" Freddy said to her, nervously.

"Yes," she replied.

"Wish they'd turn up the sounds," said Cal.

"I think it's probably just about as loud as it could go," Rosie shouted back at him.

Finally, Michael succeeded in persuading her to dance. She moved self-consciously to the beat of the music, first in imitation of those around her, and then naturally, in response to the rhythm itself. No one seemed to notice. No one seemed to care.

Suddenly it was over and they were home. Michael's mother asked how it went.

"Whew! It was pretty good, I guess," answered Michael.

"I wasn't really asking you. It was Rosie's first

138

party — and about your hundred and first. I want to know how Rosie found it. Come on, Rosie. I want to know all about it. What did they think of your outfit?"

Such a lot of fuss about nothing, Rosie thought to herself. Was there something at the party that she missed, perhaps? That others could see and she couldn't? Maybe next time it would be more clear . . . next time?

"You did enjoy it, didn't you?" Michael asked anxiously.

"Course I did. It was good — really great."

"Just as well," said Michael. "There's at least a couple of others I know of in the next few weeks. Then I thought maybe you and me could give one here, when rugby's finished. That'd be okay, wouldn't it, Mum?"

"If you say so, dear," said his mother. "Come to think of it, it does seem quite a nice idea, doesn't it, Rosie?" She smiled at them both. "Right — I'm off to bed. And you two make sure you follow my example in exactly fifteen minutes. And keep quiet — your poor father's already asleep."

"Thought she'd never leave us alone," said Michael as she left the room.

"Don't be horrible," said Rosie. "I didn't expect that she would. Your mother's lovely."

"I know, I know. Still, there's a time for mothers and a time for no mothers."

"You're just being horrible. What on earth do you mean?" Rosie asked.

He didn't answer her question. "God! You should've seen those girls' faces when they spotted

139

you! Eat yer heart out!" he chortled.

"I did see their faces. Why make such a big thing of it? I was Rosie yesterday, Rosie today, and I'll be Rosie tomorrow. The very same person."

He sighed. "But I'm the only one who ever spotted your true potential."

"If that's what it was, it took you a helluva long time. Anyway, I'm the only one who ever spotted that one day you might use words as fancy as potential!"

"I've known that word for years," said Michael. "It's on all me reports from school — usually something about me not realizing it. Not sure what they mean by that."

"You're a real fraud, Michael Geraghty. You know perfectly well what it means. Go on," she giggled, "give it a go — use another big word."

"Okay," he giggled, too. "Michael shows a distinct preference for Rosa Perkins instead of his class studies. That's been on my reports, too — except it's usually rugby."

"I'll bet."

They were sitting at opposite ends of the old kitchen sofa. Their eyes met and they stopped laughing. Michael swallowed hard, and moved toward her. Rosie's hand came up to her face and she looked uncertain, undecided. He touched her arm and she took his hand. Very, very softly, shyly and uncertainly, they kissed and each felt the gentle touch of the other's lips.

* * *

Again her father refused to enter the hospital with her to see her mother. Rosie had insisted on visiting. "If you won't take me, well then Mrs. Geraghty says she will." She secretly hoped.

"We've had enough of her," said Reg Perkins. "If you want to go, I'll take you."

This hospital was different. Not like the friendly, country hospital where her mother had first been admitted. This one was old, large and spread forever, it seemed to Rosie, across the cold countryside. She wondered why it was so isolated. So far from anywhere.

Her father seemed to know the place and directed her to where she could find her mother. There was a handful of other visitors and small islands of people dotted the very big, very bright day-room lounge. Most of the islands were quiet, silent. Tiny breaths of conversation occasionally erupted only to be eaten into a larger silence.

Edith Perkins sat alone in a corner, reading. "Hello, Rosa. What are you doing here?"

Always the same — why was she here? "Hello, Mummy. I've come to see you."

Edith put down her book. "I can see that," she said, eyeing her daughter up and down. "You look different, Rosa."

Rosie was wearing her new clothes. Her father had made no comment at all about how she looked. "They're my new things. I bought them for a party," she said proudly.

"My word," said Edith, before lapsing into silence.

141

"Are you all right?" asked Rosie.

"Shall we go for a walk?" said her mother, suddenly. "Out in the garden. It's cold but it's fine and you look warm enough. I've got my jacket here."

They walked through avenues of old trees, among flurries of fallen leaves and flower beds with spring bulbs in half leaf. For some time they walked in silence. Then her mother stopped and grasped Rosie's arm tightly as if she thought she might escape. She spoke softly but her words carried clearly on the still, cold air. "I think it will be all right. I think I will be all right. I've made up my mind this time — I *am* all right. That's what they tell me here, and that's what I am going to think — what I must think. It's important."

"Can we sit down on this bench, Mummy?" Rosie, still held fast in her mother's grip, was uncomfortable.

Her mother looked at her searchingly. "Yes. Yes, of course." She relinquished her grip and the two sat down.

"How long . . . ?"

"As long as it takes, Rosa, as long as it takes."

"And then?"

"And then it will be time for me to come home. You understand, don't you?"

"I think so," said Rosie. She was unsure. There was no full picture yet.

"Of course I'll come home. I know I'll have to come back here from time to time — probably for some years. The important thing is that now I am able to face what is wrong with me. There are

142

two things. Of course, it's the drinking — I am an alcoholic. Now, I can face that. I'm able to admit it. It's not been easy."

"And what else?"

"Not so fast, dear. Alcoholism is a disease. Put very simply it means both that I think I need, and then very definitely crave, liquor. There must be no more drink." She spoke with determination. "Secondly, is my depression. That can be treated if I give it a chance and don't double the odds against myself by drinking; because, you see, alcohol is a depressive substance in itself. It's a wonder, really, I hadn't killed myself years ago."

"But it can be fixed?"

"I'm less sure about that, Rosa. I'm told it may be controlled, perhaps that's the best I can hope for. For now, anyway, I must be willing to accept treatment. Then to see it through positively." She grasped her daughter's arm again. "You seemed to want to know. I'm telling you so that you do."

"Yes — I did want to know," said Rosie.

"Just don't expect miracles overnight, you silly little thing." Edith smiled — a wintery smile but a smile for all that. "I've thought a lot about you since I've been here, Rosa." She slipped her arm around Rosie's shoulders. "I think perhaps I'm luckier than I ever thought. I certainly have been a little blind, haven't I?"

"Perhaps," said Rosie. "I told you I cared."

"Look, Rosa, I may be making all this sound a lot easier than it is. It's all going to take time. But remember, I will try. I will."

"I want to help," said Rosie.

"As I have been trying to say, Rosa, it's because of that that I've come this far." She laughed a chilly, little laugh. "God knows, I've not been the best of mothers. I've a lot of lost time to make up. Rather lucky, I think, that you've waited so patiently."

Rosie wanted to hold her mother or be held by her. However, she made no move. Not everything would come at once. Instead, she said, "I am very happy."

"I'm glad, too, dear." Edith gave Rosie a very small, very quick kiss on the forehead.

"And Daddy?"

Edith sat thoughtfully for a time, then said, "Let's walk again. I'm a little cold. We'll have a look at their roses." She took her daughter's hand and they walked slowly back toward the hospital building. "Funny how many institutions have a rose garden. I wonder why?"

She paused by a tree and turned to face Rosie. "It is not enough, Rosa, to simply blame your father for what has happened to me. There are some things that need not concern you about my unhappiness — and about his, too. But there are also some things you should know. Your father did not make me drink. He did not keep me supplied with all those cases of liquor. I did that. If ever he did do it, it was at my insistence. Maybe, in the end, it became easier for him to comply with my wishes. Who knows? But you mustn't blame him for that. Neither was he responsible for my taking all of those tablets." A ray of sunlight came through the bare branches of the tree and shone its light on Rosie's hair. Her mother continued to hold her. "He was not responsible for that night. I did it myself. I want you to understand that."

"But you told me, Mummy — you told me he kept the pills."

"Yes, he did keep them. But surely, child, you can give me credit for being able to find them! And I did — quite easily."

"It just seemed to me . . ."

"Things are not always as they seem, my dear," said her mother. "It may be that your father has not done so very well by me. It is equally true, however, that I have not done particularly well by him. And I know full well that neither of us, your father nor I, have done our best by you. Blind drunk I may often have been, Rosa, but I haven't failed to notice his obsession with you, his . . . his . . ." She paused, searching for a word. "I don't know." She gave up. "Whatever — I think it's something you're finding very hard to bear. Well, I am as guilty for that as he is. You're young, Rosa, but you're clever. I can see that. One day, who knows, you may even be wise. And that's quite different. You do know enough now, though, to realize that everything cannot be perfect. Never count on everything being perfect."

They walked on toward the building. Rosie took her mother's arm. Suddenly, this very simple action seemed perfectly natural. "What you're saying is that not all stories have neat, happy-ever-after endings."

"Yes, Rosa — you see what I mean."

"I just wish Daddy would come and see you," said Rosie unhappily.

"Whatever makes you think he hasn't, child? Of course he's come. He has come three, four times, I think. Didn't you know?"

Chapter Thirteen

"Seems to me your football team gets to see you more than I do, these days," grumbled Rosie. "Them and your poor, dead possums now that you're out hounding them again."

"That'd be the first time ever you've said you like seeing me," said Michael gleefully.

"I said no such thing," said Rosie.

"If you want to see me more, you can come to all our games — practices, too, if you want. And I'd sure like a hand with the possums."

"I'm sure you would — but it won't be these hands. Anyway, I'm always welcome to visit your mother."

"Yeah — but she doesn't have my big charm and my cool, smooth sex appeal," he said.

"She hasn't got your big head, either. And don't start ripping off your clothes to prove a point and

147

show me you've now got six hairs on your chest!"
She laughed at him.

"Don't have to. I shaved this week, see?" He
stroked his chin and cheek.

"Is that what happened? You poor thing."

"What d'you mean?"

"Well, I thought you must have been trying to
cut your throat. How did you manage to shave
around your pimples?" she grinned.

"I haven't . . ." He felt his face. "Well, maybe
one or two."

"Pudding face," teased Rosie, quickly jumping
out of reach.

"I'll get you for that," he threatened.

She stopped laughing. "Seriously, though, I do
want to talk to you."

"Okay. Is it something I did?"

"Done," she corrected him.

"Ha! Ha ha, ha ha. Caught you that time, clever
Perkins. I done it right!"

"Did it right," she said, very sweetly.

"One day . . ." he warned. "You're just so smart.
Smart, smart, smart."

"Anyway, what I want to say is, please would
you not use your traps — your gin traps — for
the possums? I know I've said it before and I know
what you think. I know you think it's all right and
all that, but . . ." Rosie was absolutely serious.

"I can't promise you that! That's not fair. It's
not fair of you to ask. I've got my traps already,"
said Michael.

Rosie spoke softly. "I've done my homework on

148

it, Michael. There are other sorts of traps — humane ones that kill instantly."

"Yeah — and they sure cost heaps."

"Please. Please think about it. I'm not asking you to stop trapping, I'm just asking you to do it differently."

"I couldn't afford new traps," said Michael. "You know I'm saving up for a motorbike. Look. We both do economics at school. You know the story — the return I'd get on the furs wouldn't make the cash outlay worthwhile."

"There's more to it than economics, and you can afford it. If a different sort of — well — weapon costs a bit more, isn't it worth it? Isn't it better than using something you know is wrong? Your ones catch and kill or maim anything and everything. Not just possums — kiwis even."

"Rosie, there aren't any kiwis on Old Dump Road. Even you should know that." Michael risked a small smile.

"Other birds, then. And what about cats?"

"Look, if they cop a few cats, well, they'd be strays that've been dumped anyway. Damn good thing, too. You're so worried about your precious birds in my traps — I'll tell you one thing; stray cats polish off far more birds than my traps ever done. Okay, so I might've caught one or two strays but I never, ever caught a bird. So there."

"Think about it," said Rosie. "That's all I ask."

"Well, okay then, I'll think about it." He sounded unhappy. Then he brightened. "Hey! Cal wants to trap this season and he's got no traps. I'll flog

149

mine off to him, then I'll be able to go for your humane ones."

"You won't get me to bite that way, pudding face, I know your games," said Rosie. "Think about it."

"Whew! You sure can lay it on. Yeah, I'll think about it — but I'm not promising anything, all right?"

"Go home and practice your shaving," she advised, smiling at him.

Deep into July, snow fell. An unexpected and heavy blanket. Cold fronts had been coming closer for most of the month. Snow was a once in five years' — ten years' — occurrence. A welcome bonus to life in the little town. There were children alive now who had never even seen snow, never played in it.

The school and one or two businesses closed. Everyone who could got out on hastily assembled toboggans and sleds. Some strapped old tennis racquets to their boots and imagined an arctic north or antarctic south. Those who lived in the bigger houses overlooking the town dragged out skis and showed off, slithering on any small, sufficiently public slope. Snowmen were built with a hasty energy and the certain knowledge that the monuments were a test of very limited time.

On the morning of the snowfall, Rosie checked on Plum and found her huddled into a corner of her cage. Very still and quite alive, but preparing for a brief hibernation. Again Rosie dragged out the remains of the old fake-fur coat. She coaxed

Plum into action and more vigorous life. "Come on, dummy, keep moving. You're too young to seize up. Besides, if all this snow lasts more than a day I'd be surprised." She spent little time with her pet today as she and Michael had other plans. "If you want to curl up, snuggle into this. And don't moan about the bit that's been hacked out — once upon a long time ago, this old leopard saved your life."

In the afternoon Rosie met Michael. An old sled — part of a wooden door with well-worn brass curtain railing for runners — was pulled out from under the Geraghty house. It had been a few years since this treasure had seen the light of day.

"For heaven's sake, be careful," cautioned Michael's mother. "Broken limbs I might just manage, but broken necks — never." She waved them off.

The makeshift sled worked well enough and the two teenagers scooted down every slope near the house; sometimes one behind the other, sometimes solo, until the snow wore out. They finished up on the shaded, more heavily snow-drifted slope running down onto Old Dump Road. With no care for time; warm, breathless and laughing in the cold air, they slid, climbed, slid and climbed into late afternoon.

"One more time," said Michael when Rosie argued that it was late and she should be at home. "Just one more time, Rosie. My turn to steer. Come on, get on!"

They cannoned down their toboggan run of packed ice, iced grass and a patch or two of mud.

Faster . . . faster . . . faster . . . faster! Clinging to each other, laughing and shrieking, quite unmindful of the vehicle, headlights on, which was crawling its way through the icy tunnel of trees on the road below. Rocketing down their trail. Loud. Louder. Exploding at the end into a tumble of loose snow accumulated there by their dozens of runs. Head over heels. Off the sled. Rolling down. Still clinging tightly to each other. Much laughter till the final stop of tangled arms and legs.

"Get up!" The words were bullets. "Get up!" Rosie was dragged to her feet.

"Daddy!" Breathless.

"What's all this, then? Who's this?" he snarled.

"Daddy, this is Michael — Michael Geraghty."

"It's all right, Mr. Perkins," Michael found his breath, "we were just sledding."

"Get out!" The words became harsher. "Get that thing out of the way and get out of my sight!" He turned back to Rosie. "Get in the truck. *Now*, d'you hear me?" he yelled. He pulled Rosie to him, spun her around and gave her a shove toward the truck.

"Mr. Perkins . . ." Michael began.

"Get out of my way," the man growled as he headed toward the truck behind Rosie, pushing her all the while in front of him.

The sled had slithered to stop in front of a rear wheel of the vehicle. It lent traction to the truck as it revved and roared forward from its icy stop. The sled splintered into a thousand pieces.

152

* * *

"So, this is what you do when I turn my back, is it? This is what you're up to, eh? All those times I've thought you were at home. All the time. Slut! Who was that boy? Who is he? What's he been up to, eh? What've you been up to? What've you done, eh?" He was driving himself from rage to frenzy. "Behind my back! Behind my back!" Over and over again.

"Daddy, please . . ." Rosie stood, shivering with cold and terror, in the dark of the kitchen.

"Shut up! Shut up!"

"Daddy! It was Michael — Michael Geraghty!"

"Should've known. Should've known. That damned woman coming snooping round here, poking her nose in. Poking her bloody nose in when no one's asked her to. Tart clothes for you. Should've known. One of that brood, eh? Should've known. What's he done to you? Eh? What's he done?"

"Daddy!" She raised her voice. "Daddy!" She had to try to reason with him. He was moving now, moving toward her. The size of him, the rage within him, threatening. "He's done nothing. Nothing at all, do you hear me? He's my friend! Do you hear me! He's my friend, that's all. I like him."

Her words served to further inflame and enrage him. "Friend? What d'you mean, friend? What've you been doing with him, eh? What've you been doing with him behind my back? Eh? Eh? Eh?"

153

Rosie yelled back at him, "I've done nothing, Daddy! Nothing at all! Do you hear me? Nothing!" Louder still. "Can't you understand that?" Each word separately, louder than the one before. "He — is — my — friend!"

His blind rage peaked as he now stood over her. "You — you — you — you ..." He was choked with fury. He lifted his arm and hit her. First across the head in a stunning, blinding blow. And then back the other way, fingers raking across the skin of her cheek, stinging hotly. She staggered back against the table, dazed.

Her father stood, mouth slackly open, eyes glazed, panting. He looked unseeingly at his daughter for a moment, then turned, flung open the back door and left.

Rosie pulled herself slowly to her feet, dizzy, hurt and frightened. She could hear him in the garage and the sheds. It seemed to her, in the corner of her mind where it registered, that he was destroying the place. She moved to a chair and slumped into it. The noise outside ceased and she feared his return. Slowly, unsteadily, she made her way to her room and locked the door. She stumbled to her bed and climbed into it without bothering to take off clothing or shoes. She pulled the bedding over her and curled into a small, tight ball. She lay there silent, scared and shivering.

A short time afterwards she heard him return to the house. She heard the telephone ring and ring and ring. Finally it stopped, unanswered. Her head ached. It seemed swollen to twice its

154

normal size. She didn't cry. A little later, she knew by the footsteps that he came to her door, paused, then walked away again.

Finally, exhausted, Rosie fell into a fitful, wakeful and uneasy sleep.

Chapter Fourteen

The morning dawned cold, dark and grey. No more snow had fallen. What remained of the previous day's fall had iced over. Many roads were closed, dangerous and impassable. The school remained shut.

Rosie got up from her bed and turned on the light. She was stiff and cold, and her head ached with a dull pain. Moving to the mirror she examined the damage to her face and head. One side of her face was swollen, lopsided. Two ragged, red-raw lines crossed the opposite cheek where her father's nails had bitten into her skin.

She took off her clothes and changed into others, only half knowing what she was doing. She moved quietly, hoping that what little noise she made would not disturb her father. She had given no thought to what she might do. She unlocked her bedroom door and moved toward the bathroom.

Her father sat at the kitchen table, head in hands. He looked up as he heard her. "Come here," he said quietly. She obeyed and stood opposite him at the table. She could see that his rage was gone. He held out a hand to her. She trembled and backed away. His hand fell.

"Dear God," he whispered. "Did I do that to you?" She didn't answer. "Princess . . . Princess . . ." He got up and moved around toward her. She edged away from him, further around the table. "I didn't mean . . . I didn't mean . . ." Over and over. "I don't know what it was . . . it was that boy — that boy . . ."

Rosie spoke. Her mouth was dry and sore and it hurt for her to talk. "That boy was Michael Geraghty. That boy was my friend." Slow. It hurt too much. "They have lived by us for as long as . . . forever. We go to school together. We always have. He's — he's my friend."

"Princess — Rosie, I am sorry. You're all I've got. I shouldn't have done it. I'm sorry, I really am."

"I don't want to hear what you say. I want to wash my face now."

"You're all I've got. Special. Always special. My girl. My little girl." She didn't speak. "Always my girl."

"Can I go now?"

"It just came over me . . ."

Rosie didn't want to listen. She wouldn't listen. She put a hand up to her face. She felt so tired.

He went on and on and she just stood there. Kept saying he was sorry, over and over again until she no longer heard him. "Can I go now? I've got to wash my face and I've got to see to Plum. I didn't feed her last night."

He stood, his mouth working silently for a moment or two. "She . . . the possum . . ."

Her mind focused; sharply and quickly she read the signals. "What d'you mean? What have you done? Where is she?"

"The possum's gone — let her go . . ." he said, dropping his head onto his arms.

Rosie let out a scream. Tiredness and pain forgotten, she rushed from the house. The shed door hung wildly open, hanging from one hinge. All that remained of Plum's cage was a tangle of chicken wire and splintered wood.

Rosie ran, frequently slipping on the iced tracks, her throat raw from the cold. Her mind centered on one thing and one thing alone — Plum. Low branches and the winter-bare, barbed canes of blackberry added to her wounds. She felt nothing.

She climbed until exhausted and stopped on the brow of the hill. Looking back at her own house she saw the puppetlike figure of her father standing near the back door. Suddenly feeling the cold, she shivered and, eyes still on him, pulled her old jacket closer around her.

Then, pulling her gaze away from her side of the hill Rosie looked down onto the Geraghtys'. Michael and his mother were on the path. Mrs. Geraghty seemed to be embracing her son. Rosie shook her head, cleared her eyes and looked down again. They were gone. Imagination? She pressed through the scrub and undergrowth of another track and started down the hill toward their home.

They heard her coming. Mrs. Geraghty stood on the lower step of the porch. "My God!" she breathed. Michael stepped in front of Rosie on the path. The force of her run pushed him backwards and he grabbed her by the arms.

"Plum!" she cried. "He's . . . Plum . . ."

"Rosie," said Michael gently. "Rosie, Plum's dead. She was caught in a trap last night. It was one of my traps."

Norma Geraghty phoned the doctor, spoke to her husband, then called on Reg Perkins. She spent the most time on her last call. She did not raise her voice nor show any anger.

"Just for a week or so, Reg, just long enough to let things settle down. She's fine now — she is, really. You've had so much on your plate lately . . ." She reached out a hand and laid it on his. "Now, I do think you ought to pop in and see the doctor. He is expecting you — I took the liberty of phoning him. Would you do that, Reg? For Rosie's sake."

She sat with him for a long time and they talked.

Chapter Fifteen

Afterwards, Rosie asked what had happened, what the two of them had talked about. Norma looked at the girl — the battered face, the eyes that told her that the abuse amounted to more than visible, physical bruising. She chose her words very carefully.

"We talked about you, my dear. We talked about your mother, and we talked about the feelings he, your dad, has for you."

"That doesn't tell me anything," said Rosie. "What else would you talk about? That's all there is, really."

The older woman consciously arranged her thoughts. She considered the possibles and the probables and continued to choose her words with great care. It was not enough this time, she knew, to simply take the girl in her arms, hold her and offer her a haven and a home. It was not enough to allow her heart to cry out those things that she sensed Rosie wanted to hear. Rosie's stopover here would be brief, a short respite. And afterwards? Home, back home.

"Well, my little love, you'll be here with us for a wee while. Just till things sort themselves out and settle down." There would be no one else involved. She said nothing to Rosie of her quiet bullying of Reg Perkins. It had been her promise, finally, that no one else — no other agency — would become involved that persuaded him that her course of action was for the best.

"I'm going to see your mother. Your dad tells me she's very much better. As for your dad, I'm hoping he'll take himself off for a nice, long holiday, poor man — so many years with never a break. Maybe, just maybe, your mother may decide to go, too. Who knows?"

"And me?" asked Rosie.

"You?" Mrs. Geraghty smiled. "Well, my dear, like all the rest of us you'll just go on doing whatever it is you should be doing. Just as simple as that. I don't suppose for one minute, Rosie, that everything will be well overnight. Your bruises will heal quickly, you know that. What's inside . . . well, that will likely take a bit longer. You know that, too. And you must know that you can count on me, not only as a neighbor but as a very special friend. I will very certainly be keeping an eye on things." There was a definite glint in Norma Geraghty's eye. "Call me a busybody or nosey parker — whatever — but on this point I was quite definite with your dad. You're to consider this place as your second home. He knows that. And Michael is your friend for as long as you, or he, wants. Your father knows that, too."

"I love my father." Rosie spoke very quietly.

"I know, dear. And he loves you, too."

"It's just that . . ." Rosie seemed lost for words.

"Don't try to talk about it now," said Norma. She moved closer to Rosie and took the girl in her arms. "There'll be plenty of time for you to talk about it later."

"I love my mother, too. I want her — I want her better. I know I can help her get better. And I want to see her."

"You shall. I'll take you up tomorrow or the next day. But I have more than a sneaky feeling you'll soon be having her home again."

"I want that. I really do," said Rosie.

"Just — well, don't think it will all be easy, smooth sailing . . ." No point saying more at this stage, thought Norma. "I'm sure she'll be home very soon." She smiled. "Now, come on. You're going to have a rest, lie down for a while. Come on." She led the girl to her own bedroom, tucked her into the big double bed and smoothed her hair. "You just go to sleep for a little while."

"He won't — he won't . . ."

"No, love, he won't come here."

"I didn't mean that, Mrs. Geraghty. I mean, he won't be in any trouble for what he did to me?"

Norma sat down on the bed beside Rosie. "No, Rosie. No, he won't. But — and you should know this — he could well have been. Should he ever

162

again do to you what he did last night, he most certainly will be in trouble. Now, you rest."

"I — I'm glad he won't be in trouble," said Rosie.

Norma found her son in his possum shed. "I'm gonna give all this away," he said, looking around him.

"God knows I'm glad to hear that, dear. You know how I feel about it. Still," she smiled gently at him, "it's not quite the right time to make such a decision, is it? Maybe in a week or two if you still feel the same . . . Come on, now. Come inside. You can make me a cup of tea. It's not only you who's had quite a day." She took him by the arm and led him out.

Michael sat by his mother in the kitchen and she comforted him as she had comforted Rosie.

"I feel so bad about it," he said. "I feel so bloody bad."

"You've no reason to, dear."

"Yes I have. I killed her pet. Her bloody Plum. I should've knocked it on the head right back when I first saw her with it on the road. Like I was going to."

His mother looked puzzled. "Is that so?"

"Then none of this would've happened. See what knowing me has done to her? I been a blight on her life," said Michael.

"Stop feeling sorry for yourself."

"What'll happen to her old man? Will he go to jail for what he done?"

"Did, dear. And no, he won't go to jail."

163

"He should! God, I'd send him to bloody jail."

"Stop swearing, dear."

"Well, I would."

"He's her father," said Norma. "And Rosie loves him."

"Can't think why. My father doesn't go around bashing me up or anything." Michael sat quietly for a while, then spoke softly to his mother. "Like, Mum, I'm not thick or anything . . ."

"I know, dear."

"No. Be quiet and listen." He took his time and his mother listened. "Look — I know what can go on sometimes. You don't think he, well — her father, I mean — did other things he shouldn't have?"

"I don't know, Michael. Why? Has Rosie ever said anything?"

"I'd hardly be asking you if she had, would I?" Michael pointed out.

"Maybe we'll never know, Michael. And while what has happened is important, what's more important is what will happen in the future — from now on. See what I mean?"

"Yeah . . . but she's got me, now."

Why was it, thought Norma, that on this one day of her life she had to pick so many words with such care. "Yes, Michael, Rosie's got you now — at least for the time being, and that's important."

"She's got me forever, I reckon," Michael mumbled, as much to himself as to anyone.

"For now," repeated his mother.

"I need a drink."

164

"Well, then, pour us both another cup of tea."

"I meant a whiskey or gin or something," he said.

"Michael, you're incorrigible!" said his mother.

"You don't think I mean it, do you?"

His mother ruffled his hair. "Now, who am I to say what you mean and what you don't mean? But before you set out on your road to ruin, you can give your poor old mum a big hug."

In the early evening, Rosie, alone, wrapped Plum in an old, white towel given to her by Norma Geraghty. For the last time she stroked the thick, red-brown fur. "Good-bye, Plum."

Michael took a spade and together, Rosie carrying the bundle that was — that had been — Plum, they walked up the hill, across the brow and down the other side. Down to a point just above the spot on the road where she had first found the possum. The ground was hard but Michael managed to dig a shallow hole. Silently, she placed the animal in the hole and, with her hands, piled in the earth and packed it down.

Standing, she looked across at Michael and gave a small and crooked smile. "Waste of a good skin, eh?" she said.

And then he cried, tears coursing down his face. She went to him and he clung to her and she to him and her tears mingled with his.

"I never thought I'd see the day when you'd cry over a possum," she said softly.

He held her tight and said, "Bloody fool — I'm not crying for the possum. I'm crying for you."

About the Author

WILLIAM TAYLOR is the author of several young adult novels, including *The Worst Soccer Team Ever*, and *Break a Leg* (Reed Methuen).

He lives in the small town of Ohakune, in New Zealand, and is mayor of the town. A former principal and schoolteacher for twenty-five years, William Taylor now writes full time.